A

GAME   OF

CONSEQUENCES

GILL
BELCHETZ

A GAME OF CONSEQUENCES
Copyright © GILL BELCHETZ 2015
ISBN 978-1-910406-27-4

Book and cover design concept by Saatchi and Saatchi

Published by
Fisher King Publishing
The Studio
Arthington Lane
Pool-in-Wharfedale
LS21 1JZ
England

This book is dedicated to my father,
Norman Ellis,
remembered with love every day.

My dad was a wonderful man who lived a long and fulfilled life. Over the last ten years of it his mental and physical health deteriorated and he was diagnosed as having dementia. He possessed many qualities, but witnessing his deterioration from being one of life's natural communicators slip away, was the most devastating. My mum cared for him at home until he needed specialised care in a nursing home, where he died peacefully in 2014.

Dementia currently affects 850,000 people in the UK and touches the lives of 23 milllion.

A donation will be made from the sale of each copy of this book to charities leading the fight against dementia:

The Alzheimer's Society   www.alzheimers.org.uk
Alzheimer's Research UK   www.alzheimersresearchuk.org
Dementia UK   www.dementiauk.org

ACKNOWLEDGEMENTS

I am very grateful to the following people for their help in researching this book: Aisha Khan, my writing ally and friend, who generously shared her knowledge of Pakistan, Richard Armstrong for his train driving expertise, and my brother Geoff Ellis – all those hours on York station weren't wasted! Adrian Jack on Scriabin, Rob Kehoe and Richard Mindham on psychiatry, Martin Nelson about life in Mombasa, and Andrea Bell about the worries of having a child in the forces.

My development as a writer is largely due to the expert guidance of Dr. Adam Strickson, Teaching Fellow in Theatre and Writing at Leeds University – thank you for your wisdom, patience and brilliance. Huge thanks also to Kevin Roberts, Executive Chairman of Saatchi and Saatchi, who took my request for help seriously and arranged for Derek Lockwood and his team in New Zealand to design, and donate their creative concept for the cover and style of this book. You gave me the impetus to carry on.

For their advice and their support, huge thanks to my family and to my friends, who have read the book at different stages of its development and given me excellent feedback and encouragement, among you, Geoff, Kate, Vik, Sophie and James Ellis, Amy Lund, Leo Belchetz, Anne Duff, Ali and Garry Bickle, Sara Green, Michel Celemenski, Francesca Pow, Garry Lyons, Mark Catley, Sally Blundell, Sally Kinally, Lorraine and Mark Kearney, Julie Stockton, Anna Di Biasio, Connie Di Biasio, Jill Abel, Alison Hackney, Jo London, Bev Cave-Jones, Justine and Simon Somerville, Karen Crossland, Col Povey, Judy Quirke, Tim Fison, Dorothy Wyatt, John Lawton, Julie Napper, Jane Honey, and Callum

Kenny – whose help tweaking a few things was especially appreciated. Grateful thanks to Rick Armstrong and the team at Fisher King Publishing for putting so much into publishing the book and making my dreams a reality.

And finally my mum, as lovely on the inside as she is on the out, my precious girls, Rebecca and Ruth, whose love and enthusiasm through the ups and downs kept me going, and my husband Paul, who nurtured my desire to write and didn't, for one second, lose faith. This book would not have happened without you.

CONTENTS

SHAMEFACED

GIRL

For twenty minutes the train has been sitting here, no announcement, and people are getting restless. I feel pretty calm. I've been silently rehearsing what I'm going to say to my parents; I've been rehearsing it for years. To kill time I decide to do the crossword and stand up to get my bag.

I sit down again. I don't know if someone bumped into me or I'm plain clumsy, but the bag slips through my hands and the contents spill onto the floor. I scoop them up and shove them back in and then the man over the aisle, with the pale hands, points out that my book has fallen under the seat in front. I'm not bothered about the book but I'm using an old photo as a bookmark and it's one I wouldn't want to lose.

The photo was taken on my second visit to Pakistan, although my mother first took my brothers and me when I was eight. There was a plan, I later learned, that we were going to stay for good but after three months we returned to London, and my father. None of us wanted to leave. Why should we when we had an endless supply of cousins to play with, an array of tall, slim, vivacious aunts who hosted fabulous parties, and an uncle who looked like Yul Brynner. We felt more at home there than we did in England.

My grandmother's house was in Gulberg, a leafy affluent part of Lahore, and was surrounded by a huge wall. We raced around the inside of it and played hide and seek in the gardens, which were lush with giant rubber and cheese plants, and a flowering privet hedge. I remember my cousin, Asif, plucking a flower from the privet and showing me how to suck the nectar from its centre, and the thrill of the intense sweetness as it hit my tongue. When we tired we collapsed on the veranda and drank home-made lemonade brought by Siki, the maid, who had been with my grandmother for a thousand years, and our cousins teased us for our Urdu which we spoke with a cockney twang.

Some days we piled into my uncle's old Army pick-up truck and went to the Shalamar or Lawrence Gardens. We stayed all day, walking and playing, buying random plastic toys – whistles and yoyos from the hawkers, and our picnic from the carts – roasted corn-on-the-cob, ghol guppai filled with tamarind chutney and chickpeas, guavas and mangoes and ice-cream, before returning to the lantern-lit veranda to count the glow-worms and shake our heads at the stupid moths. There was nothing that first time to poison our days.

On both sides my family can trace its lineage back to 11th century Afghanistan. We are probably more blue-blooded than Queen Elizabeth II, my mother likes to say. Lineage is important. Being a good child is important. In order to be a good child one has to marry in the right place. I had just turned twenty-one when my mother whisked me off to Pakistan for the second time.

The women in the family viewed me as a project. My eyebrows were plucked and my arms waxed. I was measured and fitted for a new wardrobe and when I was deemed presentable, a first meeting arranged.

The photo is from that trip. It was taken before I met the third set of prospective in-laws. We are upstairs in my grandmother's bedroom and I am standing next to my mother, although not touching her. She is wearing an off-white shalwaar kameez and a floral dupatta made of silk chiffon, and her hair is loosely knotted in a low bun at the nape of her neck. Her jewellery is gold: two bangles, a wedding ring and flat stud earrings. You would say she looks beautiful but all I can see is the tension in her neck and the sure knowledge in her face that rejection isn't far away. I look thin and scared. My collarbones are coat hangers. I am careful not to breathe on the photo in case I disappear.

The announcement is crackly. There has been an incident, the guard says, and he is sorry for the delay. As if on cue, we all check our watches and exchange glances. An incident? We have been stopped forty minutes.

⊢ ⊠ ⊣

My aunts did their best to make it exciting and thrilling. My uncle gave me a pep talk about parents only trying to do their best for their children. I didn't believe him. Why did they wish me to marry someone I barely knew? What if I didn't like him and was stuck with him forever?

I can't remember that boy's face but I know he was tall, had a side parting which was so low it looked ridiculous, and a small moustache. I can remember the simultaneous feeling of pleasure and horror as I over-tipped the teapot and the lid fell, like a diver doing a belly-flop, into his mother's teacup.

We returned to England two days later. Take more care next time you pour tea, my mother said, before enumerating the reasons why his family were, in any case, unsuitable. I should have told her then, that I would choose my own husband if I ever decided to marry, and told my father too. In the car on the way home from the airport he made it clear that it was my mother's responsibility to secure a suitable match for me, and she had failed. She was a bad mother, he said, and she hid her face in her hands.

I got a job in a bank. Coming home from work was much like coming in from school. The minute I entered the house I knew what my mother had been doing; mowing the lawn and she smelt of cut grass, cleaning and she smelt of wood polish, and if she had been cooking, the house was full of peas, rice, cumin and onion.

I can't count the hours I watched her chop and wash spinach and coriander for the freezer, or make kebabs, the tap running slowly as she formed the mixture into little balls in her hands. And all the while we chatted. Do you know, she would say, my friend's niece has left home for an English man and she still comes back to see her mother. The shamefaced girl! There's nothing wrong with that,

I would reply, things have moved on from when you came here in the sixties! And keeping her back to me she would say, if you marry a white man, I will go to Pakistan and die there, and I will die there, I will. Or, looking me straight in the eyes, just you think what it would be like not to have a mother…

And those are the words which are running round my head when the buffet car attendant comes through the coach handing out tea and coffee and small bottles of water and I spot an ambulance and a 4x4 snaking their way across the field.

…just think what it would be like not to have a mother. And I do think about it, endlessly. It's the fear of being motherless that has stopped me, time and again, from sharing my life with them.

When I took the transfer to Leeds I said I was attending a week long course. At the end of the week I rang and said it had been extended. Six years on my mother has still not told her best friend that I have moved out. I ring her every day. I used to go home once a month but I haven't been for three. You have betrayed my trust, she says, on her more miserable days, and let me down in front of your father.

I am only preparing to have the conversation with them now because my grandmother is going to be eighty and my mother wants me to go to Lahore with her for the party. I want to go to the party – and to see my family, but not to be paraded on the marriage market. It would be fruitless. I have been married for two years.

My husband, Ed, has only ever seen photos of my parents. He dislikes the one I'm using as a bookmark and has asked me to destroy it more than once. But it reassures me. It's a kind of evidence.

There's little movement outside. The guard and buffet car attendant come through and someone shouts – have they cleared the leaves off the track yet? They stand talking at the end of the carriage, and the guard's matter-of-fact voice drifts through… the driver's in a hell of a state… they're taking him in the ambulance… the lad had his arms out, like a Messiah or something… they won't find much… the head maybe… did it bounce under the engine? Ey-up, the coroner's here. Free meals for First. Ok? Better get moving...

The coach is still. It's no stray dog or fallen tree. Faces pale. What did the guard say? He was standing on the track with his arms out... I can't think about it. I feel sick. We've been sitting drinking tea and people are outside – seeing what's there. I move away from the window into the aisle seat.

The man with the pale hands says, not long to go, and I must look confused because he laughs and says, no, not the train, you. He nods his head at my belly. Twelve weeks, I say. He looks surprised.

I open my book and stare blankly down. What about his parents, who will tell them? Their son – gone.

I close my eyes and I can see myself on my grandmother's veranda surrounded by my brothers and cousins and I am throwing my new red yo-yo away, and then pulling it back up, and they are counting each one out loud until I reach a hundred when a great cheer goes up and I fall against my mother who rubs my back and kisses my hair.

I want to hang on to this memory but my mind strays back to the dead man. Like a messiah, the guard said.

I put the photo on the table and try to smooth the creases out. I might need to show it to them.

Come on brain, think. What do I say to my parents? I've been through it a thousand times. How does it go? Do I start with Ed or the baby? Ed, no, the baby. I don't feel up to it, I'll write to them. Oh come on brain, function...

┣　薗　┫

When I come round the man with the pale hands is in front of me holding a paper bag. I have a sip of water. He says I was hyperventilating. I don't understand that. It's not something I've done before. I'm sorry if I've caused any trouble, I say.

The train starts moving and a few people cheer. I spin my wedding ring round and round. Just you think what it would be like not to have a mother; no mother. I will go to Pakistan and die there – and I will die there – I will.

No mother – just think…
I run my hands over my bump. I will be that shamefaced girl.

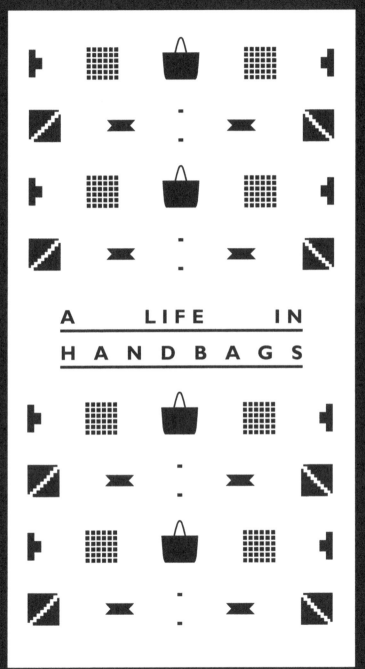

A   LIFE   IN
HANDBAGS

Frank comes home with a brown leather suitcase: he's bought it brand new from Russell's. It was an extravagant act but he can't have you going in with anything shoddy. You pack it and put it by the front door. It contains toiletries and night-wear and baby clothes: some old, some new, and some hand knitted. Nothing blue, because you're secretly hoping for a girl. Nappies are provided and you've less than a month to go.

You wake in the middle of the night lying on a cold wet patch. You think you've peed and lumber out of bed. When you stand the fluid pours out and you give a little scream. My waters have gone, you tell Frank, and calm as anything he gets things sorted and drives you in.

Nothing is too good for my girl, Frank says, and he pays six shillings a day for an amenity bed. He's sent home by the midwife and you're left to get on with it. It takes twenty hours until you're rewarded with tea and toast and a nine pounder called Andrew.

You follow the breast-feeding instructions on the back of the wardrobe door and remarkably the baby thrives. For ten days you rest up and the evening before you leave you're given a lesson on how to bath baby.

Frank swaddles Andrew and puts the Moses basket on the back seat of the Morris Minor. He flings the case in the boot. For the first time motherhood dawns on you and Frank stops and lets you weep out all your anxiety. It's going to be all right, he says and when you get home you take control of the baby and Frank takes the case down to the cellar, where it grows a fine layer of mould.

Your second and third pregnancies end in miscarriage. When all hope seems to have gone, Sally is born.

I ☒ I

You remove the Hermès alligator bag from the top of the wardrobe. Frank brought it back from a trip to London, never thinking it would have its only outing at Andrew's funeral more than thirty years later. You've never cared for black.

You do your face with your usual degree of precision, tinker with your hair and lacquer it well. Sally brings up tea and shortbreads from the round tin with soldiers on it: the buttery smell sets you off again and you empty the bilious dregs from your gut into the toilet.

The subdued voices of people you don't want to see drift upstairs. Only Frank and Sally can share your grief: not your sister and her family, and not Frank's brother, who has unexpectedly returned from Kenya. None of them know what it's like to be visited by the railway police at 11.09pm on a Saturday night.

It's time to go. With the Hermès bag over your arm and your head held high you go down. In the car Frank grips your hand until you think the bones are going to break, and Sally cries.

Since the news was delivered, the dreadful-dreadful-what-a-waste-of-a-life-news, your thoughts have become vague and filmy and your sentences are often without ends. Will the church…, will the flowers…, will the food…?

The church is bitterly cold. The new vicar does a passable job. He keeps the prayers short and sums up Andrew's life in eight minutes. In fact, he skirts around the details quite nicely, and almost implies that Andrew has been eaten up by cancer, rather than a train. You interpret the Vicar's ambiguity as sensitivity but can't warm to the man.

The service is over and you follow the coffin into the rain and on to the crem. Frank and Sally hang their heads and shut out the world. You peer into the gloom, not believing it will ever lift. It's the only time you've seen Frank cry and it's heart-breaking.

I ☒ I

You go out whilst Frank is in the back garden pruning the roses. It's a sunny day and you wear a yellow cardigan. Yellow isn't a colour you usually choose, but lately you've developed a penchant for it.

In the shopping mall a lady stops and says Hello May. You smile at her brightly and ask How's – how's... but for the life of you can't remember her husband's name. Jack, she says helpfully, He's fine. The encounter leaves you feeling out of sorts. You can't remember her name either, or where she lives, and think that this not remembering thing is a blooming nuisance.

You go into The Magpie Café. The waitress brings over the usual. No handbag today May? she asks, and you look around and realise that no, you haven't got a bag, and now that she's drawn it to your attention, being without one feels very strange. Have this one on the house, she says, and pats your shoulder, which you don't care for. The thought of buying a handbag makes your armpits burn.

Next door is the charity shop. You mooch around and for a while feel like your old self, picking out garments, feeling the texture of them. You pick up a brown handbag. It's made of shiny plastic and is unlike any handbag you've ever owned. The lady behind the till says to drop the money in later. On the way home you take a wrong turn and walk for a mile until a police car pulls up and the young man offers you a lift.

You put your shiny brown £3 handbag on the kitchen table. Frank looks at it in horror. I wish you wouldn't go off like that on your own, he says. You feel cross. A mask sets on your face and you gather up the bag and go and sit in the lounge. You ignore Frank until the next morning when you wake up and have forgotten all about it.

⊢ ䷓ ⊣

A roomy green canvas bag with pink lilies woven into the fabric sits by your feet whilst you nap. Sally bought it especially for Luxor. Every now and then your limbs jump and your head slips forwards. Frank puts his hand tenderly on your forehead to hold it back so you won't wake yourself. After twenty minutes you stir and lazily trawl the room.

You ask Frank where you are and he says you're on a cruiser going to visit a temple. Well, that's news to me, you say. You spot the floral canvas bag, pick it up and rummage. You pull out a tube of hand cream and beam contentedly, and then the bag slips down your stockinged legs and spews its contents over the wooden floor with a disturbing clatter. Your lipstick, loose change, powder compact and polo mints race around the wooden deck. The rest make a little mountain by your feet. A shrill voiced lady tells you not to worry and kneels down to help. You catch hold of the handle and snatch it away from her. She looks offended, but you don't give a fig.

Frank tells you softly to steady on and asks if you want to go back on deck. You look puzzled, so Frank, who has developed the patience of a saint, explains again that you are in Luxor, on a cruiser, going to visit a Temple. That's news to me, you say. Frank smiles and kisses you softly on the cheek. You hold out a hand and let yourself be led up into the sun.

| 茵 |

You hang on to a glossy patent leather bag in babydoll blue that Frank bought to salve his conscience. He stops the car outside a building that looks familiar, but it won't come to you. Where are we? you ask. Look at the daffodils, says Frank.

He helps you out and you go inside and wait. You feel the tension in his hand and want to go home. We can't love, he says, and pretty soon a lady with a round face and a big smile calls you through.

This is Dr Langdon, says Frank. Do you remember Dr Langdon, she goes to our church?

You don't. Frank's mouth is set in a fixed smile that makes your tummy flutter. The lady from church asks if she can check your memory out. You grip the patent bag and glance at Frank but he's looking the other way. Oh, you say.

You know you are English and live in Leeds but don't know the year, the day, the date or the season. The church lady asks you to remember three words: fish, house and bread. You repeat them: fish, house and bread, and then she asks you to write your name on a piece of paper. You hold the pen and write the letter M. You stop. No more letters come. Can you still remember those three words I mentioned earlier? she asks. Words. Earlier. You look confused. I'm an idiot, you say, and then Frank leans over and through watery eyes he says, You are not an idiot, and more loudly, Do you hear, you are not an idiot!

⊦ ☲ ⊣

A net bag with over large holes hangs from the Zimmer frame. A big leather purse and a hanky embroidered by your sister with the letter M are caught in the net like a couple of unlikely fish. You walk into the frame, move it forwards and walk into it again. It takes six minutes to get from the bedroom to the toilet where Frank helps you twist round and sit down. You perform and he comes back and cleans you before following you slowly to the bathroom.

The shower is the perfect temperature. Frank is careful to get you good and clean and takes care not to wet your hair. The warm water is soothing and when Frank helps you out, you purse your lips and wait for his kiss. After last night, when you pushed him and hit him with more strength than he'd imagined possible, he's pleased to feel your lips against his: the smallest sign of love, of recognition or gratitude, is better than none.

You cling on to the frame whilst Frank pats you dry and generously talcs you, leaving a ghostly white film under breasts and arms, down your back, between your legs and over your feet. Haltingly, you walk back to the bedroom draped in a towel and sit on the bed whilst he dresses you. He doesn't bother with your bra anymore. You flinch when he lifts your right shoulder, which is still bruised from the fall you can't remember, and he slips on a pink non-crease blouse. He puts your cardigan on, drops a skirt over your head, rolls on your pop socks, fastens your shoes over swollen feet, and then holds your hands and helps you stand so that he can pull up the padded knickers and straighten and tuck everything in. He fastens the string of pearls he bought for your pearl wedding anniversary around your neck, and brushes your hair. From the dressing table he offers you a range of lipsticks and when you fail to point to one, he picks out his favourite, coral, and puts it in your hand. Without hesitation, which amazes Frank, you dab it on your lips and smack them together. There you are, pretty as a picture, he says, and prepares himself for the once daily palaver of getting you safely downstairs.

Every third day Frank shaves your chin and repaints your nails, which don't chip like they used to.

What Sally says is true: Frank cannot manage any longer. The home has a vacancy but he has to let them know by 5pm. He makes the call and an ambulance is booked for Friday.

Downstairs in the cellar Frank finds the brown leather case. He cleans and polishes it until it looks like new, and when he weeps, tears bounce off it like a cloud burst on hard baked earth.

OUT OF

HOLBECK

Once a fortnight Jim visits Pete. He goes because of York station and Tulyar: he goes because they share a passion for trains.

He pops his head in the front door, shouts hello to Pete's dad and goes round the back, swallowing the bitter saliva that has flooded his mouth. In the minute it takes to reach the garage the memories of the day he and Pete met, swamp his brain. They lift him: the power, the smell, the surprise and raw excitement; and they crush him. Unable to move, he stands with his hand on the door and stares into the bubble wrapped windows. He can see himself, with absolute clarity, on the first Reliance bus out of Stillington, checking his gear.

In his bag he has a cagoule and a thin balaclava, two rounds of spam sandwiches with tomato sauce, two packets of salt and vinegar crisps, two Wagon Wheels and a can of coke. He takes his binoculars out, slings them around his neck and studies his Ian Allan Trainspotters' Guide. The names alone are enough to bring him out in goose pimples: Meld, Tulyar, Alycidon; the racehorses of the train world. He pores over a picture of a huge class 55 Deltic. The driver is shielded from view behind small tinted windows which are set up high like threatening eyes on a robot's face. Mesmerised, he traces its outline with a reverential finger.

The bus stops in Exhibition Square. Jim gets off and runs to the depot where he has a quick scout round for anything interesting. By 7.43am he's on platform eleven. He knows the exact time he arrives because the clock at York station is both huge and accurate. He's on his own for a spell but at thirteen he's veteran enough to know that the best view of trains from the South is to be had from the end of platform eleven, and that others will soon come and muscle in on his space. He gets his binoculars out.

A brand new rucksack slams down next to him. He turns around and frowns.

'Seen anything good?' asks a tall lad who sits down a few feet away. He has well scrubbed cheeks and oozes cleanliness.

'Nope,' says Jim, which isn't true: he's already copped a Peak and two English Electric Class 40's, but he can't be bothered with a newcomer. Tall lad looks crestfallen.

'I'm goin' up t'other end,' says Jim, and he gets his stuff together and heads off over the footbridge.

Platform one is heaving. Jim's eyes dart about checking for anything unusual: a Class 25 on a parcel train, a Class 45 Peak from Newcastle, but it's all pretty regular stuff.

Over the din the tannoy booms, 'The next train into platform one will be the 08.32 to London King's Cross calling at ...' His heart races. He hears the drum roll of the engine before he sees it and as it draws nearer the platform vibrates, and when the front draws level with him and he can read the head code, he runs along side until it grinds to an inelegant halt with a series of clanks and crunches and a shattering squeal of brakes. The noise on tickover is obnoxiously loud.

'It's a racehorse,' he says to no one in particular. 'It's Tulyar – Tulyar.'

At the top of the engine's steps stands the second man, a young lad not much older than Jim. The driver appears behind him.

'Can I look in yer cab mister?' Jim shouts.

'All right son,' says the driver. 'We've had a good run from Newcastle and we're runnin' a few minutes early – hop up – be quick.'

From outside the cab looks tiny, claustrophobic even, but from the driver's seat a vast exciting world opens up. The rails run away, clean strong silvery lines caught in the winter sun. Jim drags his eyes inside. He doesn't want to miss a single detail: the worn metal handbrake marked ON and OFF, the miniature windscreen wipers, the pinned-up sun visors, the circular gauges, the big knobs, the small knobs, the buttons, the lights, the metal foot plates and best of all, the sign in the middle: MAX SPEED 100MPH, in red on a white background. One hundred miles per hour! He must be dreaming.

'She's called Tulyar,' the driver says.

'Aye,' says Jim, 'she won the Epsom Derby in 1952.'

The driver's big throaty laugh fills the cab and he cuffs the top of Jim's head with his gloved hand. 'Come on,' he says, 'yer three minutes is up.'

Jim reluctantly slides out of the cab and the Deltic accelerates away. The noise is more highly pitched than any other engine. It has more in common with a Grand Prix car, thinks Jim. The sulphuric smell of diesel saturates the air and lingers long after the train has vanished. He inhales deeply: it's better than his mum's perfume.

'Did ya see that?' a voice comes at him. It's the tall lad with scrubbed cheeks.

'Copped it and cabbed it!' exults Jim.

He turns away and skips off. At the end of the platform he stops and looks back. Tall lad is rooted to the spot, slack jawed, wide eyed.

Jim catches an early bus back to Stillington. He licks the chocolate off the outside of his Wagon Wheels but they don't taste quite as sweet as they should.

⊢ ▣ ⊣

Jim pushes the garage door open. Pete comes towards him and claps him on the shoulder, leaving a lick of red paint on Jim's tee-shirt. Jim always wears the same shirt for these visits.

'How are you mate?' asks Jim.

'Better,' says Pete, and he takes Jim's arm and pulls him into the garage. At the back is an old wallpaper table littered with essentials. Jars of scatter ballast contain snow, coarse turf and fine turf. There are tubes of PVA glue, tiny paint brushes and pots of paint. Pots and pots of paint from Signal Red to Fluorescent Signal Green, and a host of chipped saucers and plates used for mixing. In the middle of the room is a ninety-foot model railway on a board measuring 12ft. by 8ft. The canal is Humbrol 157 Azure Blue, the houses 113 Rust and the grass 131 Mid Green, and the tracks are edged in spidery lichen: orange, green and ochre. There are black and white cows too.

It is superb but slightly strange in some respects: Newark Station sits opposite Holbeck Shed and the Leeds Liverpool Canal runs through the middle. Numerous engines sit on the sidings, including Tulyar, and there are three bridges, a small school, a church and a couple of dozen houses on Aire Street.

⊢ 🎲 ⊣

Aire Street is deserted. Jim forces himself to walk slowly but even so, he's the first of the twelve new trainees to arrive. The last to come is a lad who has to bend his knees and duck his head to get through the door. Jim hangs back: the memory of his meanness two years earlier bites him. Tall Lad comes over and throws a scruffy rucksack down on the chair beside Jim.

'You bastard. I was sick as a dog that day you cabbed Tulyar.'

Jim's guts churn. He holds out a hand.

'Sorry mate,' he says, and to his relief, Pete grabs it and squeezes it tightly.

'Accepted,' he says, and laughs a happy open laugh.

For the next six weeks they sit next to each other and soak up the joys of signalling, coupling procedures, boilers and rule books – there is nothing in existence as fascinating as a train and all its paraphernalia.

They walk to work from Hunslet where they rent rooms from a driver. When they aren't at work they are in the snug of The King's Arms listening to stories: the failed level crossing, the stray dog, the hapless child swinging her legs over the edge of a platform. They are only stories: embellished and gruesome. It won't happen to them.

For seven years they work as second men out of Holbeck and eventually they get a shot at the driver's course. The new two car trains are little more than glorified buses but they are elated nonetheless, and content – until the intoxicating lure of electrification comes to Leeds.

Why settle for Hebden Bridge at 55mph when you can have London at 125mph?

Pete lands a job in the cab of a Class 91 carrying seven hundred folk a time to London. Jim doesn't mind. He's wrapped up in the preparations for his wedding to Dawn. To celebrate Pete's promotion they go to Harry Ramsden's for fish and chips.

▐ ▣ ▐

The garage is brightly lit.

'I'm going to do it today – whilst you're here,' says Pete.

'Brilliant,' says Jim. 'Go for it.' He stands back, knowing full well what will happen.

Pete places a small plaster figure on the bench by the field of cows. The man is wearing white clothes and has flowing hair. He looks like a messiah, but he is no saviour.

'It will be ok today,' says Pete. 'It will be ok. I've got the colour right. The hair – it's a mix of 62 Leather and 63 Sand. It will be ok.'

Pete turns on the power and the Class 91 moves forwards. It runs around the perimeter of the track thirty times. His hand hovers over the controls. If he flicks the switch it will direct the train across the middle, past the Friesian cows and the man on the bench. With each circuit of the train the beads of perspiration on Pete's brow multiply. He dries them on the sleeve of his uniform.

Jim holds his breath; Pete's becomes laboured and the acrid smell of sweat fills the garage.

'What if he does it again?' Pete asks. 'What if he stands on the track and I can't stop the train and …'

'It's ok mate,' says Jim softly. 'He won't get up. Lightening doesn't strike twice.'

Pete's shoulders shudder: frustration leaks out of him. He collapses against Jim who comforts him as he would one of his own children, waking from a nightmare.

When Pete regains control he has to tell the story again. He speaks with slow deliberation. He stops between sentences and pauses. He checks at each stage that he's remembering correctly, searching for something that might have warned him. Jim knows it word for word.

'It was quiet. I went up to the 5th floor and booked in. There were no emergency speed restrictions so I went down to the train and put my key in. I did the safety checks. The doors closed and the blue interlock light came on. I got two on the buzzer from the guard, moved the reverse into forward, gave the guard two back and opened the power controller. I kept my eye on the traction light and as soon as it was orange, I let off the brake. Doncaster, Retford, Newark – and at the flat crossing I put her into full power and we flew around the bend. We went past the cows and I could see for three hundred yards. There was nothing. I swear there was nothing. And then I saw him, standing with his arms out wide and I shouted 'Mooooove.' But he didn't. I shouted it again. 'Moooooove.' I slammed the brake into emergency and I saw into his face. I looked clear into his eyes, and his lips were moving and then – slam. Into the train. Slam – and he got eaten up. It took a mile to stop. I wanted to go back – to check if he was alive but they said the spoiler had ripped off his arms and his legs and his head was pulp. And they laughed...'

Jim leads Pete into the house and sits him at the kitchen table. Pete's dad makes a pot of tea and they chat about football and the weather and the price of beer until a kind of normality returns.

'I'll shut everything down for you mate,' says Jim, and he goes round the back. The hum of the train making another circuit infuriates him. He picks up the seated figure and grinds it to dust between his fingers.

'Miserable bastard,' he says, and cuts the power.

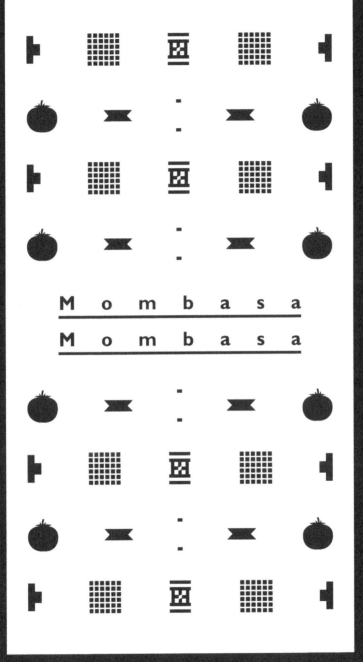

MOMBASA MOMBASA

Joe retired after forty-four years in the law and three years later Millie died. It wasn't fair. You work hard all your life, spend hours mapping out your retirement, come home from the Wednesday afternoon French class and find your wife slumped sideways on the downstairs toilet with her knickers ballooning over her ankles. An ugly death at an ugly time. Family and friends formed a cocoon around him.

'It's going to be hard Dad,' said Harriet.

'Life's shit,' said Jack.

The mixture of concern and pain in their faces was too much so he went to stay with an old friend in Mombasa for a month. That was four years ago.

┠ 亞 ┨

It's February. It's 6pm, dank and dark. He lets himself in and picks up a few letters from the mat. The cold is already seeping into his bones. He's flown back for his nephew's funeral so will take the opportunity to see his kids and grandchildren, visit his financial advisor, and sort a few things out. He wasn't surprised when his brother rang; he always thought the boy was weak. He drags his case across the hall, humming the word Mombasa to himself – Mombasa, Mombasa, Mombasa – over and over again, and smiles. He loves the sound of this word, its palms and coconut and heat. He shouts it out into the stairwell as he heads upstairs.

He sets a bath running and, knowing he can afford to leave it ten minutes, calls Mombasa. Cheered by the call he quickly undresses in the bathroom, takes two white flannels from the cabinet and steadies himself on the taps as he clambers in. He washes himself systematically: face, neck, feet, legs, stomach, arms, backside. He throws the flannel into the sink, heats the second one and lies back and puts it over his face. The warmth is like a poultice for his jagged nerves.

How is he going to handle tomorrow? What will Harriet say when he tells her?

A jet of acid shoots up and burns his gullet. He cuts the bath short and chews on a couple of antacids. Wrapped in a towel he sits on the bed and picks up the phone to call his daughter. He puts it down. He'll have something to eat first.

⊦ 🔲 ⊦

The family home is a groaning affair. After all these years mean streams of air still catch him unaware and leave him chilled. He puts the kettle on and takes a loaf out of the freezer. The butter's solid so he puts it in the microwave. He tells himself it will be okay tomorrow and rolls his head to ease the tension. He and Harriet get along well – they speak every Monday at 11pm, Mombasa time. The phone rings.

'Harriet, hello. I was about to call you and you've beaten me to it – yes the flight was on time – well almost. Are you still alright for tomorrow?'

The minute minder pings on the microwave and he opens the door.

'Oh hell! – What? Good – it might be better if it was just the two of us – there are a few things I want to talk to you about – no, nothing serious. Around eleven then? Bye. Bye.'

He stares at the pool of butter.

The rest of the evening is spent in the barely warm kitchen. He sits on a tall stool at the Formica peninsula writing a list and sipping Glenmorangie. The kitchen, the whole house, needs gutting. Funny how he never noticed that when he was living there full time: it had seemed pretty splendid to him then. He looks up a few phone numbers and adds them to his list. It's not too bad – reorganising one's life in eight easy steps. He drains the glass and heads off to bed. He feels his seventy-two years more acutely in the evenings.

He falls into a deep sleep. At 4am he gets up for a pee and when he lies back down Millie whirls about his head. He can't get her out no matter how hard he tries until, exhausted, he gives up and walks around the house looking for peace.

At 6am he showers and unpacks. He takes the presents he's bought for his granddaughters downstairs and puts them on the sideboard in the hall. The two black brightly beaded dolls stand ten inches high and have big happy white smiles painted on their faces. He smiles back at them and lines them up so that the girls will see them as soon as they arrive.

After breakfast he starts making calls. He ticks his way down the list and writes the appointments in his diary. By mid morning he's done and the butterflies in his stomach pick up. He makes a strong Kenyan coffee and goes upstairs to wait for Harriet. When the bell rings he feels sick.

They sit in the kitchen immersed in talk about the impending funeral.

'Anyway, I'm pleased you've come,' Harriet says. 'I didn't think you would.'

'I couldn't not come...' says Joe, trailing off.

They watch silently as a large yellow skip is set down in the middle of the drive.

'A skip Dad?'

'Yes.'

'You're having a clear out at last then?'

'No – well yes – it's a bit more than that actually – I'm putting the house on the market.'

'Oh!' Harriet looks away and twiddles her hair.

'I'm going to start looking for an apartment near here. I want to keep a foot in England,' says Joe.

'A foot in England,' says Harriet quizzically.

'I'm going to spend more time in Mombasa. I think the sun's good for me.'

'We hardly see you as it is,' Harriet laughs. 'Any more and you'll be in danger of going native.'

It's quiet for a moment and then Harriet says, 'How much time?'

Joe gets up and washes his hands.

'I don't know. Nine, ten months of the year possibly.' He keeps his back to her.

'Is that wise?'

'Wise? You're questioning my wisdom?' says Joe turning round and eyeing his daughter, but Harriet doesn't back off or cower like she used to; she holds her father's gaze.

'Yes, wise. It's on the news all the time – people hacking each other's arms and legs off...'

'Hey hang on,' says Joe. He wipes his forehead with the tea towel and throws it on the table. 'It's not like that.'

'What! They're lying?' says Harriet.

'No. In some places it is – but not Mombasa. Kenya's a huge country; it's localized trouble and it's virtually over.' This isn't going well. 'Look,' he says in a softer tone, 'I wouldn't stay there if it wasn't safe. It's as safe walking in the streets there as it is here.'

Harriet shrugs. 'I'll take your word for it but you can get sun in Europe you know. What's wrong with Portugal?'

'Nothing. But I like Mombasa. You don't understand what it's like.'

'Make me understand then,' says Harriet.

So he does his best to make her understand. He tells her about the fruit and veg shop which smells overwhelmingly of fresh earth and of the assistant, Henry, who greets him by name and selects the best of everything (melons, carrots, paw paw, sweet potatoes – the list is endless) and about Bititi, who wears a brightly coloured kikoi and has tightly plaited beaded hair close to her scalp, who weighs them and reckons up the total on a calculator slower than he does in his head, and how Henry carries them to the car and how he gives him a small tip because that's how it works and that there is always a happy banter between them. And the tomatoes cost 20p a kilo. And how he then goes for an upmarket cappuccino at Café Moco at Cinemex, with a piece of lemon cake on the side. And from the balcony of his second floor apartment he gets the soft warm sun from 6.30am as he looks out across Mombasa harbour onto lush vegetation: acacia, palms, mangroves and the baobab tree, and small colourful parrot like birds sing and steal crumbs. And the fish, they call it haddock but it's not haddock, is the freshest and tastiest ever. And his weekly visit to the Mombasa club, a private club, which is so cultured in a post colonial African kind of way. And barbeques, on Sundays, a group of them with children, at the posh hotel where for a small backhander they use the pool and have sun loungers all day.

All of this tumbles out of his mouth as he paces up and down.

What he doesn't tell, because he can't help his rose tintedness, is how he once caught a glimpse into the filthy rotting back yard of the veg shop and how the children wait outside, ragged, dirty, selling nuts or hard boiled eggs and a man in a wheelchair begs so he gives him 20 shillings (130 shillings to the £) but he wishes he hadn't because another ten arrive. And the pavements are lined with men selling their wares or their trade, plumbers with pipes, electricians with wires, but he wouldn't trust them an inch. And how there are bars around the apartment and security guards and mosquito nets and noise noise noise all night because noise is good and Kenyans argue loudly and are afraid of quiet and the meat is tough because it isn't hung. Oh, and the overcrowded ferry and the corrupt politicians and the aggro of visas and how if he needed surgery he would come back to England.

And after he has finished Harriet says, 'What about your grandchildren? You won't be a part of their lives,' and Joe, carried away by his eloquence says, 'I've taken on an African family, a ten year old and a 4 month old, as one does.'

'As one does?' says Harriet.

'Yes. You have a sister, Aminah, she's with her mother right now – my partner – Halisi. She's twenty six.' He pulls out a photo from his top pocket, of Aminah and Halisi in their colourful attire and hands it to Harriet who studies it.

'What about Jack,' she says, staring at her father. 'Does he know?'
'Jack? Your brother? Yes.'

She shakes her head. 'You didn't come for the funeral at all,' she
says, and drops the photo. She stands up slowly and walks out of the
kitchen into the hall. Joe shouts after her but she keeps on walking
and swipes her hand at the dolls as she passes.

The removal men have most of the house empty by lunchtime. The
large oak sideboard in the hall is one of the last things to go. It takes
four men to move it. When it comes away from the wall a black doll's
head drops onto the floor and rolls into the corner by the radiator pipe.
The new owner's daughter finds it. She has never seen a black doll's
head before and is thrilled. For a couple of days it's her favourite thing.

NO   TIME

FOR   PICASSO

On the train in from Roissy Alice put her feet up and leant her head against the window. She twisted slightly and pressed her temple harder against the icy glass. It felt strangely soothing and she stayed like that for a few stops until a French couple got on with a young child. She thought the child was about six, seven maybe, but she wasn't very good at guessing children's ages. The child, a girl, was dressed in a thick winter coat: it looked expensive, designer even. It was at odds with the parents' coats which were made of a faded felt material. Hippies' coats, thought Alice. Maybe they weren't the child's parents. Maybe the child was abducted. Alice shut her eyes and tried to ignore them. She was getting ridiculous.

The train filled up as it made its way through the Parisian suburbs. Alice glanced at the child intermittently. She was standing by the doors tracing a pattern on the glass. Her finger was following the narrow trails left on the outside where rain had made rivulets in the grime. She was completely absorbed in what she was doing. The adults, Alice didn't like to think of them as the child's parents, were pointing up at the map of the Metro, disagreeing about something. The train came to a halt and the doors slid open. The child kept her arm raised and her finger pointed, waiting for the doors to close so that she could resume her game. Suddenly, a new idea seemed to strike the girl and she got off the train and stood on the platform examining the window from outside.

'Monsieur, vôtre fille est...' began Alice.

The man spotted the girl and as the warning bell sounded he threw himself between the closing doors, which slammed into his body and shot open again. He grabbed hold of the front of the girl's coat and yanked her off her feet and back inside. The woman, who was still seated, now sprang into action and set about berating the child, who looked back at her forlornly. Fellow passengers 'O là là'd' and gesticulated, their disapproval palpable. An uneasy calm settled in the carriage and at the next station the trio disembarked. Alice watched the back of the girl's bright coat disappear. She felt sad for the girl and indignant towards the adults. She also knew that her feelings were rooted in jealousy; she longed for a child of her own. Yesterday's funeral had left her feeling edgy and unsettled in a way that she hadn't anticipated.

The hotel was tucked away on the left bank. It was still early, and the plan was that Alice would join Graham in bed for breakfast. They had been having an on-off relationship for six years. It was on, when he was away attending a conference and she was able to tag along, and it was off, when he was at home. Usually, the prospect of seeing him would fill her with an impatient excitement, but today she walked slowly along the side of Notre Dame. It was mid February and the sun was barely warm. She was thinking about their previous Paris trips. Each time they had stayed in the same hotel and each time, she now realised, had been less good, less satisfying, than the previous ones. Graham's wife Marcie, who he claimed to have lost interest in before their honeymoon was over, had produced a son between each visit, three in total. Alice really couldn't remember when the talk of him asking Marcie for a divorce had finally petered out.

She picked up a room key at reception, took the lift to the third floor and let herself in. He was standing looking out of the window: the excess flesh on his waist pouched over his hips; his buttocks, which always struck her as too big for a man, were pink. He spun around when he heard the door close and cupped his hands over his genitals. They were large hands but they failed to conceal the mass of red pubic hair that spilled out around them.

'My my, you look guilty,' she said, and dropped her bag on the floor. It was a discreet brown leather bag, small enough to pass through as hand luggage, and it landed with a dull thud on the thin carpet. She glanced round the room. It was one they hadn't stayed in before and it was verging on shabby.

'What took you so long?' he drawled, in a fake French accent. Alice didn't feel in the mood and shivered when he moved towards her. She couldn't find any comfort in his arms.

'You're freezing,' he said.

'And you're boiling. Is the bath still in?'

She topped it up and lay back. One bathroom had begun to look much like another over the years. The first bath they shared was in Florence.

They met by chance looking at Bacon's portrait of Henrietta Moraes in a Manchester art gallery. He made some comment about it being little more than wallpaper, Alice disagreed, and he moved away. When she stopped for a coffee he asked if he could join her. He was a natural conversationalist. He liked art, had a dog and was a surgeon, but the most striking things about him, apart from his red hair and pale aqua eyes, were his fingers, which were long and tapered. The nail ends were of an equal length and were creamy white. When he caught her staring at them she felt as if she'd been caught out somehow.

A fortnight later she met him by the statue of David in the Uffizi at 2pm. They hadn't even kissed. After Florence came Venice, then Madrid, Prague, Paris, Berlin, Rome and Paris again. Europe began to feel exhausted.

Graham knelt down by the side of the bath and cupped one of Alice's breasts in his hand. She was going to tell him about the incident on the train and then thought better of it: he would bring his own children into the discussion and she didn't feel up to it.

'Do you mind if we make love later?' she asked, putting a hand on top of his.

'No. Later's fine,' he said, but his clipped voice let her know other-wise. 'Don't be long,' he said, 'or we won't get tickets.'

⊦ ☲ ⊣

Outside, on the banks of an almost frozen Seine, they walked purpose-
fully towards the Grand Palais. Alice liked Paris. Out of all the European
capitals she had visited it was the one in which she felt most at home.
When she left school she worked for six months as a nanny for a French
family on the Rue de Rennes, where, from her tiny attic bedroom, she
spent hours examining the minutiae of the Paris skyline. Now, as she
walked along, she picked out the familiar landmarks. The Eiffel Tower
was ahead to their left, to their right, the vast river frontage of the
Louvre and in the distance, the huge glass dome of the Grand Palais,
shone silver. Alice estimated it to be about twenty minutes away at the
pace Graham was setting. There was nothing leisurely about Graham;
he was a man who cracked on with things.

He marched her onwards. The briskness of the walk loosened his
tongue and he talked about the exhibition and how well it had been
reviewed. Alice listened with half an ear and wondered if Marcie did the
same thing, nodding now and again, just enough to convince him she
was still interested. Her mind was back in the packed church. There
had been many backs of heads that she hadn't seen for three or more
years and at the end she slipped out quietly to avoid accusing eyes. In
the car on the way home huge sobs burst uncontrollably out of her,
forcing her to pull over until she regained control. She wasn't a woman
who cried, but suicide left you reeling.

Their progress along the Seine was impeded by a young woman
who Alice didn't notice until it was almost too late. She was dressed
in dark earthy shades and was crouched down on the ground rooting
for something. Graham sidestepped the woman and pulled Alice out
of her way, but before they could get fully past the woman caught hold
of the hem of Alice's coat.

'Look, look,' she said. 'It gold, I think it wedding ring. It you wedding
ring? You husband ring? You drop it, no?' And she held out an arm with
a chunky gold ring in her palm. She spoke with a heavy French accent.

Alice and Graham stared at the ring.

'She's not my wife,' Graham said and laughed a little awkwardly. You bastard, thought Alice.

'It my lucky day,' the woman continued. 'It gold, look at mark, you see, it gold, no?' She thrust the ring under Alice's nose. Alice looked at it. She could see the mark but it was the woman's slender fingers and dirt encrusted nails that drew her eyes. Graham saw them too. He was fastidious about nails.

'We haven't got time for this,' he said

The woman smiled. Her teeth were the colour of cold tea. Alice closed the woman's fingers around the ring. She felt pleased for her good fortune.

'You take it,' Alice said. 'It's your lucky day, not ours.'

'No, no,' protested the woman. 'It too big. Look.' And she slipped the ring up and down her bony finger. She put it in Alice's hand and walked off. Alice looked embarrassed. She made as if to follow the woman but Graham tightened his grip on her hand and dragged her on. They hadn't walked more than ten meters when the woman came up behind them and tapped Alice on the shoulder.

'You keep lucky ring and you give me Francs, yes?'

The ring felt inconceivably light in Alice's hand. It didn't matter that it wasn't gold.

'Oui, bien sûr,' said Alice. She reached into her bag for her purse.

'Are you mad?' said Graham. 'It's a con for God's sake.' Alice ignored him. She took two hundred Francs out and gave them to the woman.

'You are mad,' said Graham, his eyes steely. He shook his head uncomprehendingly and walked off. Alice could see that the woman knew she was responsible for their spat and that it fleetingly crossed her mind to give the money back, but she glanced at something beyond Alice and tucked the money firmly in the pocket of her jacket.

'C'est pour vous,' said Alice. 'Bonne chance.'

A little further on two young children waited expectantly on a bench. Their cheeks had the grey-green complexion of a duck egg, and an air of fragility hung over them.

I 亞 I

Le Grand Colbert was on the Rue Vivienne. The food was unquestionably excellent and it was a favourite of Graham's. Their table was at the far end and afforded them an excellent view. The room was long and heavily mirrored, and was draped with velour curtains of the deepest red. Potted plants – on a scale too huge to imagine, sat atop the stainless steel counter, and above the bar, row upon row of sparkling glasses hung down and a pile of lemons perched precariously. Posters advertising Tante Olga at the Théâtre de la Huchette, lined the walls, and the waiters, dressed in black jackets with velvet collars, moved with pride and purpose. At the door, the Maître d' turned away a stream of hopeful diners. Alice took it all in: she wouldn't be eating there again.

At a nearby table a chic middle-aged woman was comforting a weak looking man who was crying. Alice's husband wept when he begged her not to leave, and now, he was horribly gone. She felt crumpled inside.

Graham cut through her thoughts like he had cut through her life.

'You've been a bit odd today,' he said.

'What,' said Alice. 'Odd because I gave money to a woman and her kids who were half starved or odd because I didn't want sex?'

'Odd on both counts,' he said, and returned to the wine menu.

The man at the nearby table stopped crying and Alice felt relieved.

'Too bad we couldn't get tickets for Picasso,' Graham said.

'You can go early and queue tomorrow morning.'

'Are you not coming?'

'No. I'm flying home,' said Alice.

'That's up to you but you won't get to see all those paintings together again.'

'I'll live with that,' said Alice. She looked down at his bleached hands resting on the starched white tablecloth. She would miss his hands. If it wasn't for his wedding ring, you would hardly have known they were there.

Wendy re-read the coroner's letter. It was barely two weeks since she last saw Andrew. She felt shocked and saddened. He was her patient for twelve years: three admissions and a host of outpatient appointments, and she liked him, genuinely liked him, and his parents too.

The usual questions came to her: Is it my fault? Have I missed something? Experience told her it wasn't, but that didn't count for anything. She rang Ella and asked her to find Andrew's medical records.

Whilst she waited she wandered around the office. It was huge now that it was almost cleared. On the back wall were seven pictures, her architectural CV, as she liked to think of them. They were mainly of the psychiatric units she'd worked in – dark Victorian institutions or prefabs, but the one on the left was taken by her father on the day she qualified and showed her standing in front of the old medical school, a wide grin on her face. Usually it made her smile but the news about Andrew put a pall on what was always going to be a difficult day. She took it down and leant it against the wall. She stacked the others up against it and sat down heavily, her mind a jumble…

Of all the people. Andrew Hastings. She thought he'd turned a corner – and yet he took so much care to get it right. He was one of her success stories.

Ella came in carrying a huge set of notes.

'Two o'clock,' she said brightly. 'You won't forget or disappear will you?'

Wendy looked blank.

'Your retirement party?'

Panic overcame her. How could she listen to speeches lauding her career when failure marked the end of forty years in medicine? How cruel, when there was no time left to rewrite the ending.

'Don't let this ruin today or cloud everything you've done,' said Ella. Wendy reached a hand out to her.

'You've always been able to read my mind,' she said.

⊢ 亘 ⊣

She took the first set and rested her hands on top. Hours of interviews to read. Medicine charts to pour over. It felt pointless. Was Andrew a metaphor for her career? Had she been fooling herself that she was better than she was? She shook her head. Oh, get on with it, she told herself firmly.

The first entry was what Wendy privately referred to as 'Scriabin night.' She thought she remembered it clearly but reading the notes she realised that much of the detail had disappeared: the time of night, the house, who else was present…

It was after midnight when she got to Harold Terrace. There was a police van parked outside. With one foot out of the car she stopped and listened to the music coming through the broken window. Scriabin, Number 8 of the Opus 8 Etudes, was being murdered by someone.

The house was a red brick back-to-back, a two up two down, built before the war. It was probably meant to house a small family, or a grand piano, but not both. Wendy stood with her back pressed flat against the door and quickly worked out who was who. She knew the GP – a half-witted woman who couldn't make decisions, and the social worker, but the others were new to her. Trying to hide in the alcove was a middle-aged couple. The man was hollow-cheeked with fatigue and he held his arm protectively around the woman. He was pressing her face into his shoulder, so that only her hair was visible, pale gold, against the grey of his jacket. Wendy instinctively knew him to be a good man and felt the familiar urge to help. Furiously playing the piano was a man wearing a bobble hat. Andrew Hastings, she presumed.

He didn't notice Wendy's arrival. He carried on playing, his left hand striding up and down the keys, his right splitting notes. It was a hideous sound but none of them moved. When he finished, he overturned the piano stool and pushed the arm supporting the lid sideways so that it came crashing down. The woman in the alcove let out a wail and buried her head further into the man's shoulder. The Social Worker and GP backed into the kitchen. Wendy winced – it was a Steinway D-model. She took a step forward and offered Andrew a hand. He ignored it.

'I composed that piece myself,' he said in a grandiose voice, 'and I'm going to play it for the Queen. She's on tour with The Duke of Edinburgh in The Caribbean and as soon as I've packed I'm going over there to play it for them.'

He paced round the piano sliding his left forearm over the top, as if attached by some magnetic force. When he came to the fallen stool he took an extra long stride. He had the wide-eyed look of a baboon.

'I'm going to fly on Concorde. Queen Elizabeth told me to come first class. The Presidents of America, Chile and Germany all want me to play for them. They make good sausages over there.'

'Andrew...'

He skirted past.

'I must pack now or I'll be late for the ship. I'm going on the QE2. I have to get to Southampton you know.'

A relative calm descended. Wendy introduced herself to the couple, who were Andrew's parents. She got out the forms and signed them with the GP and social worker. Chat was kept to the minimum; it was 2am.

Andrew bounded down the stairs bare-footed, carrying a ruck-sack over one shoulder.

'I'd like you to come to the hospital so that we can have a chat,' said Wendy.

'No. I'm fine. Absolutely fine.' He made a small bow and flicked the tails of an imaginary jacket out of the way before he sat down. 'I will play you a piece I wrote yesterday. Look here.' He pointed to the name at the head of the score of music. 'It's all about the four seasons.'

He was well into autumn when the Ambulance arrived.

⊦ 亙 ⊦

Wendy turned each page, wondering what she would find next. It was a relief to see that the notes were detailed, written longhand the following morning. Several more entries followed describing Andrew's progress as his mania was brought under control. So far there was nothing amiss. Her first proper meeting with Frank and May Hastings was also clearly recorded.

Frank was a large man and he spoke with a soft Geordie accent. He clearly loved his son and it was he who told Wendy about Andrew's life, as he saw it, about him being a Boy Scout and a music lover, about his sister, Sally, and his friends, and how he changed at university. The Scriabin episode took them by surprise.

By comparison, May Hastings was tiny. She must have been around sixty then and was a beautiful woman. Pale blonde hair framed her face and her skin was pale too, as if it had never seen the sun. She sat quietly, holding on to the navy patent handbag on her knees, and let Frank do the talking. When Wendy got to know them better she realised that this wasn't because she was afraid to speak, or felt she should defer to Frank in any way, but because she was happy that what he said was true and represented them both. When Frank had said all he wanted to say, the room fell quiet and they could hear Andrew playing the old upright piano in the common room. May flicked the gold clasp on her handbag up and down and finally asked, 'Will he ever be completely better?' It was a question Wendy had been asked a thousand times and she wished she could give them the answer they wanted.

The thought of May and Frank made her shudder. The least she could do was speak to them. May answered the phone. Wendy couldn't refuse her request to meet and they agreed upon twelve midday. She put the phone down and wondered what she would say. She was used to talking to bereaved relatives but rarely became as involved with patients as she had with Andrew. She gave an irritable shrug and returned to his notes. There was no point rehearsing.

Ella showed them in. They accepted Wendy's condolences with quiet dignity, and as they sat down May let go of her husband's arm and took hold of Wendy's, clinging on to it tightly. They didn't deserve this, and for the first time Wendy felt anger towards Andrew.

'The funeral was on Wednesday,' said Frank softly. 'The church was full.'

'I'm not surprised. He was a fine man.'

'A fine son,' Frank agreed. He smiled bravely.

May's hair was like filigree; she pushed it away from her face. She leant towards Wendy and stared into her eyes.

'We saw him the evening before he... he seemed a bit brighter. We thought he'd turned a corner and was starting to get over...'

Alice's name hung in the air. Wendy received an invitation to their wedding. They were an odd match.

'We should have made him come home – when she left – so that we could help him more. We didn't help him enough,' said May.

She began to cry and Frank pulled her towards him. They sat awhile and then Frank said, 'We have no one to play the piano now.'

'Did you know that the staff on the unit used to call Andrew the piano man?' said Wendy. 'When I went to see him he was often playing the piano, and how well he played was usually an indication of how he was progressing. Nobody could play Scriabin like Andrew...' Her voice broke. May pulled away from Frank and reached in her handbag for a hanky. She passed it to Wendy who wiped her cheeks. 'I'm sorry,' she said. 'It's me who should be comforting you.'

They fell into a melancholy silence that was eventually broken by Frank.

'Are you moving offices?' he said.

'Retiring.'

'Oh! We won't see you again.'

'Yes you will,' said Wendy. 'In the Coroner's Court.' Frank looked relieved. 'Anytime you want to talk you can call me. Anytime.' She paused. 'You know, Andrew was unwell for many years. If any parents did enough, in so far as we can ever do enough for our children, it was the two of you.' They looked at her from their hunched over position, soaking up her words. 'You have nothing to blame yourselves about,' she said.

It was after 2pm when Ella came looking for Wendy. She was feeding paper into the shredder.

'You don't need to do that,' Ella said.

'I want to.'

'How did it go?'

'Badly? Well? I don't know. It never gets any easier.'

'Can you face the party?'

'No.'

'But you will?'

Wendy nodded. 'I'll be ten minutes at most. I'll follow you down.'

⊦ ⊠ ⊦

She opened the notes and flicked through them again until she reached their last meeting. Andrew was pre-occupied with Alice and said she'd been seen at the Coliseum in Rome with another man. Wendy wrote that she thought it was most likely one of his flights of fancy, but apparently not. She closed the records and put a big elastic band around them. There was to be no complete severance from work. The details would natter until the serious incident review and the inquest were over. Everything would be gone through with a fine-tooth comb.

The desk drawer was empty except for a spare lipstick. She painted her lips and dropped it in her handbag. Two empty chairs were by the desk and May's umbrella lay on the floor. She picked it up and then let it fall.

She fanned her hands out over the wood-wormed surface of the beautiful oak desk and tried to tot up how many hours she'd spent sitting at it. Too many, that was for sure, yet now it was time to leave she couldn't find the impetus to move. The night at Harold Terrace was vivid, refrains of piano music hammered inside her. She first heard Scriabin played by John Ogden at the Wigmore Hall. She could hardly forget it; it was the night Mike proposed. He bought what he called 'connoisseurs' seats,' in the middle of the mahogany balcony, because they were less 'boomy' than the stalls. The audience gave a standing ovation for Number 12 but Wendy thought Number 8 was better. He played with such delicacy and intensity of feeling that it reduced her to tears. She felt tearful again now. Andrew and retirement – it was too much for one day.

She suddenly wanted to see Mike. At breakfast when she questioned her decision to retire, he said, 'In that hospital, no one is irreplaceable.' After the party he was taking her out for dinner. It would be somewhere memorable. That was Mike all over.

A tap on the door reminded her where she should be. She stood tall and straightened her dress.

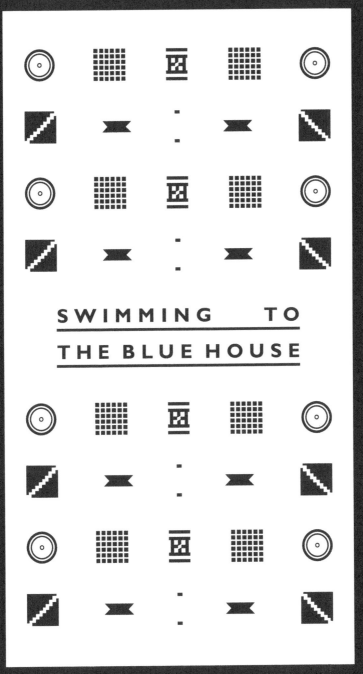

SWIMMING TO
THE BLUE HOUSE

The taxi driver was huge. His head was squashed down into his shoulders and he swung it from side to side and back again. His eyes, which Sally could see in the rear view mirror, looked permanently upwards; only the whites were visible. He was a hairy man: thick tight curls on his head gave way to short bristles on his neck and hair sprouted from the back of massive hands that gripped the battered steering wheel. Sally asked him to put the meter on and he ignored her.

'I tired,' he said and poked his big tongue out of his mouth.

Sally felt slippery between her knees, down her back and in her armpits. She checked for marks. There was the beginning of a stain and she blew down the front of her dress, flapping the fabric to circulate the air. The driver caught her eye.

'You go on own?' he said.

She looked out at the parched landscape. It was nine months since her brother's death and they had been marked by lethargy. What she was doing was crazy, and risky, and God knows what the vicar, who dropped by twice a week to stare at her breasts, would think, but her desire to be with Hassan overrode these thoughts and she dismissed the driver as interfering. At thirty, she was past being told anything.

The driver broke hard and Sally groped in her purse and pulled out a large note.

'Shokran. Shokran,' he said, his eyes full of gratitude.

She slammed the door. He watched her walk off with the dark skinned man who was probably from the south: he had the broad nose and wide lips of his Nubian ancestors.

Hassan was waiting outside The Sonesta Hotel wearing jeans and a faded red tee shirt. Sally thought he looked less trustworthy out of his tour guide uniform and the apprehension she felt before leaving the hotel resurfaced. He held her hand and led her into a side street. She took long strides to keep up with him and tried to remember the route they were taking.

'It this one,' he said.

There was no door on the apartment block. Sally followed him up the rough concrete steps, breathing hard, stopping briefly between floors to look out of the broken windows onto the rubbish filled pit below. On the sixth floor he unlocked the door and let them in.

'It hard to get anywhere, even for few night,' he shrugged.

The door closed and he covered her mouth with his, thrust his tongue in and out and bit her top lip and then the bottom. Sally's heart pounded. His hair felt springy under her fingers.

'Condoms?' he said.

Sally looked blank.

'I go for condoms. Lock the door and don't open it.'

She wandered around uneasily in the silence, feeling excited and terrified. The flat was a grimy unclean space: bare carpets, dirty sofas, a bedroom with a large bed carelessly strewn with a stained cotton throw; no sheets. She found the bathroom and used the pink toilet, which wouldn't flush and had no lid. The taps were empty and she'd left her wet wipes back at the hotel. Outside, a car pulled up. She peeped through the slatted blinds and saw two men jump out. One stood smoking, idling, whilst the other used the street phone. She took slow breaths to quell her anxiety and then looked in the wardrobe.

Hassan returned with condoms and two large bottles of water.

'Don't drink the tap water,' he said, opening a bottle and taking a swig.

'There isn't any,' said Sally.

He took her hand and pulled her into the bedroom. She stood by the bed and watched him take off his shirt and unzip his flies and push his jeans down to his ankles. His shoulders were narrow and his skin hair-free, save for the mass of tight pubic hair at the base of his belly. His penis was long and narrow and stood flat against it. He looked up.

'What you wait for?' he said.

She pulled her knickers down and her dress up over her head. Her weighty breasts hung on her belly, and her thighs, like young seals, covered the bed. It didn't matter that she was fat; he fell on her greedily. He sank his hands into her flesh and squeezed. He gnawed at her nipples and moved jerkily, pushing his erection hard against her thigh. Too soon, he rolled on a condom.

The ceiling was sapphire-blue and rippled. Flakes of paint had come loose revealing lighter patches, and like the Nile at dusk, it shimmered, and she imagined herself swimming across it – kicking her legs out wide to reach the blue house on the far bank. But the house wasn't getting any nearer, and although she kicked harder and stretched her arms her energy drained away, and as he heaved in and out, the Nile became a cracked ceiling once more.

He slid off; his penis naked.

'Good eh?' he said.

He pulled on his pants and went into the lounge. She could hear him speaking Arabic on the phone – calling his friends, or the men she had seen through the window, telling them to come round, maybe. The feeling of panic surged up from her toes and enveloped her. The doorbell rang. She pulled on her knickers and dress and picked up her shoes and bag and shoved past Hassan and a man in a white jacket, out into the stairwell. At the bottom she put on her shoes and could hear him shouting from above. She ran into the empty street.

The landmarks she memorised earlier had vanished. The buildings and streets merged into an anonymous mass and she ran and walked and stumbled until she finally stopped on the rough ground by Luxor Temple. A row of human headed sphinxes stretched out in front of her and a single obelisk towered above. Transfixed, she stared into the eyes of Rameses II and wondered at her madness.

Someone was shouting. Again, shouting, from a car. She scanned the gloom and recognised the taxi driver's hairy hand hanging out of the window.

Lying on the back seat she wiped her face on the hem of her dress and licked the salt off her swollen lips. She kept her eyes shut until the taxi came to a halt.

'No pay. No pay,' said the driver, still rolling his head from side to side.

She left the notes on the back seat and walked through the foyer, avoiding the knowing eyes of the doorman.

The water came up to her chin. The pungent orange oil from Luxor market formed chaotic circles on the surface that bumped into one another each time she moved her knees. On the floor lay her knickers: the condom had fallen out of her and into them. The thought of Hassan being inside her, made her feel sick.

When the water was cool she got out, flicked the condom into the toilet and dropped the knickers in the bin. She carelessly dried herself and wandered into the bedroom. She sat on the edge of the bed and looked down at her orange-stained breasts. What will the vicar make of them, she wondered?

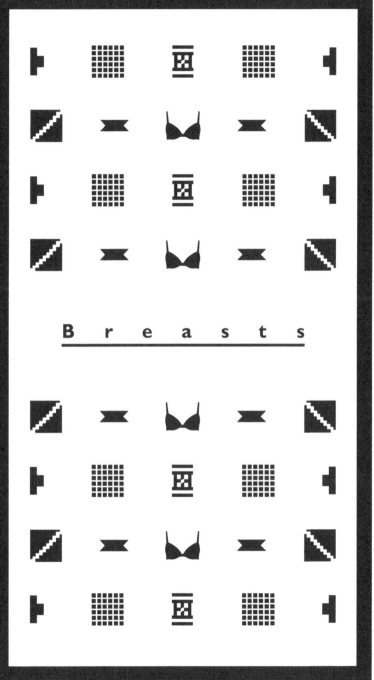

B r e a s t s

It was not just the size of them, but their bounciness. When she sat down they carried on vibrating, as if they had their own secret energy supply, and he wondered what it would be like to hold his head between them and inhale deeply. With some reluctance he chased the thought away and presented her with his deepest sympathy smile.

'Some tea to warm you?' he said.

It was as though she hadn't heard. She gazed out towards the snow-covered lawns, immersed in her own thoughts, eyelids fluttering lazily. He took off his specs and studied her. He noticed the large brown beret that hid her hair, the milky skin and crook nose that dominated her face, but it was her body that excited him and his eyes lingered on it. She was abundantly and gloriously fleshy, so much more of a woman than the starveling who modelled at life class. She was a Fernando Botero and he wanted her to strip off and lie on the sofa so that he could paint her, capture the light on...

'No thanks,' she said. 'What do you want to know?'

'Whatever you want to tell me.'

Her eyes were sorrow-filled. He pushed a box of tissues towards her.

'I don't know what to tell you – I've no experience of anything like this.' She spoke loudly.

'Of course you haven't. Was your brother older or younger than you?'

'Older. Obviously.'

The tears spilled out. With each sob her shoulders forced her breasts closer together. He let her weep.

The crying unlocked her and she talked quickly, repeating the same few details over again.

'There you have it,' she said at last. 'His life in half an hour. Pitiful really.' By now the beret had been discarded and strands of hair stuck to the side of her face. She pushed them back irritably. 'If you need anything else you'd better let me know. Can you think of anything?'

He heard her by the back door cursing as she tussled with her Wellies, and watched her walk down the drive, hat back in place, coat pulled tightly round her, trussed up against the weather. The Vicarage felt lifeless. He looked at the few notes he'd made. Not much to go on: Piano-player, Boy Scout, divorced, dog; hardly enough to make an appreciation of any worth. He would have to resort to his bank of platitudes, talk about the all-consuming sorrow felt by family and friends and encourage them to look to God to help make sense of this death – not that he would mention the nature of death – he would give them a palatable version of the truth; imply that he'd been prematurely taken by an illness which none of them could have done anything to prevent.

He poured himself a whiskey and sat down at his desk. He drew two large breasts with coat-hanger nipples on the blotter and began to write. He used brown ink and gained immense pleasure from seeing his untidy scrawl fill the sheet. It took less than ten minutes and when he was done he read it through and slipped it into a plastic wallet. He took a white label, stuck it on and filled in the man's name, Andrew Hastings, and the date of the funeral. It was far from personal but it would suffice. It would have to, because his mind was already back with the girl whose breasts he was colouring in. He needed to see her again. A home visit, a week or two post-funeral, would be the answer.

He had no difficulty finding her house, which overlooked the park. He picked his way through the slush and went to the side door. It took three knocks before she answered.

'No cold callers,' she shouted.

The irony wasn't lost on him.

'It's Reverend Good.'

'Oh!' A pause. 'I'll find the key.'

The kitchen was a mess. She looked a mess. The lounge was worse. She cleared a small space on the sofa for him and squeezed herself into the armchair opposite.

'You were the last person I was expecting.'

'I hope I'm not intruding. I saw your father on Sunday and he was concerned about you.'

This wasn't strictly true. He'd made an ungodly dash from the nave to the door to ask her father how things were and was told they were 'managing.'

'What's your name?' she said.

'Richard.'

'Do any of your parishioners call you Richard?'

'You can call me Richard.'

She tutted. 'I didn't ask you that Richard, but I suppose they don't, do they, it would no doubt be unseemly for them to call you by your Christian name.'

She leant over and picked up the newspaper from the floor. Her breasts leapt forward, almost out of her loose pyjama top, and then jostled for position when she sat back. Surely she wasn't unaware of what had happened? Was she testing him?

'Here,' she said. 'You'll know this. Seven across. Ishmael's mother. Five letters. I thought it was Sarah, blank-A-blank-A-blank, but then four down couldn't be Sheath.'

He wasn't a crossword doer. He was picturing her reclining on the sofa, one arm above her head, the other supporting her lower breast, her knees...

'Well?' She looked at him impatiently.

'Hagar,' he said, some silted-up region of his brain rousing itself.

'Sarah was married to Abraham and when she couldn't have children she suggested that Abraham father a child for her, with a slave girl called Hagar.'

'H A G A R. Brill-ee-ant.'

He moved to stand behind the armchair from where he could get a better view. Within five minutes they had it finished and she threw it on the floor with a false jubilance.

'The highlight of the day,' she said. 'How sad.'

At his Wednesday night life class he found himself unusually dissatisfied with Nina who was sitting naked on an upright chair. He sketched quickly, in charcoal, stopping to smudge the contours of her meagre body, trying to soften the bony edges, but it wasn't working. She was wrong. The light was wrong. He wanted a huge canvas and a model with amazing craters in her flesh that would demand great gobs and whorls of paint. He wanted her bounciness. He left early.

On his second visit they talked about her brother. She'd been down to the railway to see where it happened. When the first train passed she caught the backdraught and vomited into the long grass. He asked her if she felt guilty. 'Yes and no,' she said, but wouldn't be drawn.

They talked about her mother too, who was worryingly forgetful. It was all on her shoulders now – it always had been.

'That's boys for you,' she said, with an almost bitter smile.

Visits fell into a Monday/Thursday pattern. She was signed off sick and didn't envisage returning to work in the near future. She was a librarian at the university, a job she disliked. She called herself a Luddite, said it was changing too fast and for the worse.

She was always in pyjamas. He liked the baggy ones that allowed her heavy breasts to swing freely. The pink florals were his favourite. They were missing a button.

She was rarely out of his thoughts: delivering a sermon, talking with the churchwarden, painting Nina. And at night he dreamt he could feel her lolling stomach and magnificently generous form beneath him. He couldn't help it and didn't want to help it. When his wife left, sometime towards the end of his months of treatment, he hadn't believed he would feel this kind of schoolboy infatuation again and he feasted on it.

┝ ☴ ┥

The vicarage garden was a mass of overblown daffodils. He picked a bunch of light and dark and took them round. He hadn't taken her a gift before and was surprised to find his mouth felt claggy. He thrust them into her bosom.

'I'm vaseless,' she said and abandoned them on the draining-board. He checked the kitchen cupboards for anything that would do, a measuring jug or a pint glass, and finding nothing suitable emptied out the teapot and crammed them in, the ache of disappointment spreading. He thought about going home but she wanted to hear his Easter day sermon, so he stayed.

The theme was conventional, the structure with its repeated juxtaposition of life and death persuasive, and he hoped it would soften her atheistic views. She sat in her usual chair, legs tucked up as far as the flesh allowed, and crooked her head. He warmed up quickly. Free from the pulpit he felt liberated and paced around waving his arms. He reached his favourite line; 'To die is to fall into the hands of the living God,' and glanced at her. She was trembling with suppressed laughter. Tears were rolling down her face and a tiny whimper escaped her body as she keeled over sideways.

He grabbed her by the shoulders and shook her, like you would someone who was choking.

'It's not you,' she said between gasps. 'It's what you said. It's nonsense, religion. It's no better than witchcraft.'

He binned the daffodils and made tea in the pot. Apologies came quickly but their conversation was brittle and he stood up to go.

'Where are you going?'

He took it as a measure of her remorse that she was asking: she was rarely curious about his life.

'Art class.'

'Art class! What do you paint?'

'Naked women,' he said. 'I could paint you if you'd like.'

She looked sceptical. Her mouth opened and closed and it pleased him to see her lost for words.

⊦ ▨ ⊦

Nina was having surgery and a new model came. Derek. He was altogether ordinary and unable to hold a pose. The classes lost their appeal.

⊦ ▨ ⊦

One day in early August he was surprised to find her smartly dressed.

'I've been summoned to Occupational Health to see if I'm better,' she said. 'Any chance of a lift?'

It was six months since her brother's death. Mentally she was stronger, but all the same…

'That can't be right. It's far too soon.'

She had a mulish look about her.

'Of course I'll give you a lift,' he said.

She filled the front seat. Her thigh spilled out over the hand brake and when he reached to let it off his hand disappeared under the warm flesh. Twice in three miles she chastised him – for going through a red light and for clipping a kerb.

He watched her walk into the building and imagined he could hear her bare thighs rubbing together. He dug his fingers into the pad of fat at the base of his neck and tried to relax. It was hopeless. He was overwhelmed by her invisible presence, by the earthy smell which lingered in the car, and the thought of her slipping away was unbearable. Maybe he could persuade her to pose for him, every Wednesday night, just until Nina was better?

The meeting with the doctor went well. Her return to work was scheduled for the end of September and prior to that she was going to take her parents on a holiday, somewhere none of them had been before, somewhere hot, like Egypt: a cruise down the Nile, perhaps.

'Have you time to run round by a Travel Agent?' she said.

It was less of a detour than he thought, so his proposition was cut short. She was pre-occupied, drifting off into one of her fluttery eyelid states, and he didn't know if she was taking him seriously or not.

Ⅰ⠀☒⠀Ⅰ

He took them to the airport and two weeks later picked them up.

Sally was in a good mood. Her face was tanned but the mound of flesh that escaped her bra had a puzzling orange tint.

She saw him looking.

'Bath oil,' she said, and blushed.

Egypt was superb. The Temple of Hathor was vast and remarkably intact, the sunrise over the Valley of the Kings, splendid, and the Nile, well, so much more than a river. Excepting May's confusion, the holiday had been a success.

Ⅰ⠀☒⠀Ⅰ

Her mood changed when she returned to the library. He wanted to ask if she'd given his proposal any thought but she felt nauseous and was distracted and the timing wasn't right. In the event, he didn't have to ask: she rang one afternoon and said she was ready if he wanted to bring his things round.

He found her lying on the sofa in a scarlet negligee. It clung to every abundant contour and was inviting and terrifying.

He ignored the direction of the light and set up his easel, dropping brushes and tubes of paint, spilling water on the carpet. The visual measurements he usually took, the distance from head to breast, waist to hips and knees to feet, went by the board in his rush to get started, and using a thick piece of charcoal he set about sketching the curve of her back and the line of her arms. He sketched loosely and when she didn't fit on the paper he rubbed out and corrected until she did. When he was as satisfied as he was likely to be, he brushed over the charcoal with water to remove the excess and waited for it to dry.

'Can I go to the loo?' she said.

He wanted to put sticky dots on the sofa to mark out her position but he found the proximity of her near-nakedness intimidating, so held back, and whilst she was gone he painted in a green background and squeezed dollops of paint onto the board.

She returned and made herself comfortable, and then, he dared to move closer and adjust the lie of the fabric and the spread of her hair.

'Do you mind?' he said tentatively, taking a handful and trailing it down the length of her neck.

Gradually she became texture, light and shade: her skin a mix of orange red and white, her nipples purple hued, hair and eyes brownie black, and in a broad red slick from crimson to claret, the negligee hugged her body. But his concentration was incomplete and it bore little resemblance to her. He left it drying on the easel and went to wash his hands.

She came to him in the kitchen and placed her bare toes on the tips of his shoes. He looked at her, with his head slightly cocked, as if seeking permission. He saw the laughter in her eyes and when she didn't speak he slid the straps off her shoulders. She smiled and closed her eyes. Softly, he touched the underside of her breasts with his fingertips, and then, unable to wait any longer, he gathered them up in his hands and lowered his head into the luxurious chasm between.

It was over dinner on St Swithin's day that she told him.

'You're going to be a father,' she said, a tremor in her voice.

He looked confused.

She carried on dishing up the Shepherd's pie.

'We're going to be parents. I didn't want to say anything until I was sure. I did a test this morning.'

He didn't doubt her pregnancy. For a second he allowed himself to believe he was the father of this child, to believe that a miracle had happened and the chemo hadn't knocked his fertility for six. He looked at the painting which was still on the floor. It was no Fernando Botero: it probably wouldn't make it to the wall, but he had the real thing now, and he couldn't imagine a time when he would tire of her abundance. He reached across the table for her hands.

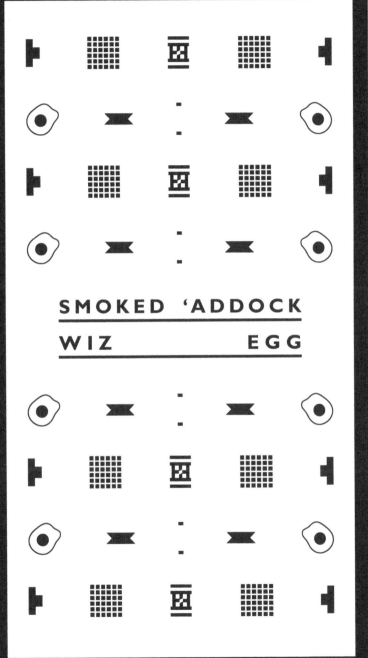

SMOKED 'ADDOCK

WIZ   EGG

SMOKED 'ADDOCK WIZ EGG

Alice was there on a whim. No. Not a whim exactly. At this time of year it was an idea that got into her brain and stayed there, rattling around like the refrain of a bad song you want to forget but can't. Round it went, hooked in, except this year she hadn't been able to chase it out. So here she was at The Admiralty. Checking faces. There wasn't much going on in her life at the moment.

She slipped off her plum-coloured suede stilettoes, 'fuck me shoes,' her best friend called them, and massaged some feeling back into the balls of her feet. She hadn't planned to go in the gallery but once she was there she couldn't resist: the paintings at The Courtauld were too good to miss and she didn't get to London much any more.

The waiter brought the menu and Alice smiled her thanks. Still the same. Still an elegant classy affair, swirls of letters hand written in tawny brown ink on a thick sheet of icy green paper. She ran her fingers and thumbs over its smooth surface rubbing them up and down rhythmically, trying to remember how many years she and Graham had met there on the last Thursday before Christmas. Six? Seven possibly? Funny how details she thought she would never forget had vanished. He used to joke – although you'd never call Graham a joker exactly – that she remembered every mouthful she'd ever eaten. She didn't, but the smoked haddock thing was different all together, and it happened here.

'Madame?' said the waiter, cutting through her reverie.

'I'm sorry,' she said and quickly searched the menu.

'Chef recommend ze fish of ze day, 'alibut.'

Alice wasn't keen on fish but now that he'd suggested it she found herself asking for smoked haddock with a softly poached egg on top and a glass of Australian Sauvignon Blanc.

The waiter looked perplexed. He was a young man, in his early twenties, dark haired, slightly cocky. He spoke with a heavy accent.

'But we don't 'ave smoked 'addock on ze menu today Madame.'

'Would you be kind enough to ask the chef if he would cook some – if he has some – please? It... it would be a real help if you would...' she trailed off.

'Certainly Madame. I will ask chef. It ees no problem to ask,' and he turned briskly on his Cuban heels. Less than a minute later he was back. 'Chef is veree 'appy to make you smoked 'addock wiz egg,' he beamed.

Alice took a sip of wine, closed her eyes and held it in the well of her mouth for a few seconds. It was dry but full, and when she swallowed, herby flavours tickled her throat. It was good. 'Up yours Graham,' she thought. He was such a wine snob. He never chose wine from the new world: he derided their scientific approach, said they didn't understand the importance of land, of terroir. 'Bollocks to that,' she said, raised her glass in a toast and took a slurp. The fish was slow in coming so she ordered another.

'Make it a large,' she called after the waiter.

When was it she ate the haddock and egg exactly, at Christmas or some other time? Not that the date mattered. What mattered, was that it was an example of how she capitulated to his wishes – no, demands, that was a better word. Wine, exhibitions, where to meet. Sex and food. He knew she didn't like eggs but forced her to order the haddock with the egg. He would have said something like 'Your taste buds will have matured since you last tried a poached egg,' in a patronising tone. So she did, and it ended in disaster, the half-chewed contents being spewed noisily into a serviette, eyes streaming. Call himself a doctor? All he did was look on, a horrified expression on his face. She could have died if the bloke from the next table hadn't whacked her on the back.

Why had she stayed with Graham so long, she wondered? Always on the brink of leaving Marcie, never quite doing it. Babies, Marcie's not hers, popping out every couple of years. Cheaper hotels. Less thought. Maybe she should have stayed married to Andrew after all. She suddenly felt very lonely, utterly unhappy and empty, and she drifted into a kind of stupor which was broken only by the reappearance of the waiter who, with exaggerated ceremony, placed the fish in front of her with a look of triumph.

'Your 'addock Madame,' he paused, 'wiz softly poached egg.'

Alice mumbled a 'thank you' and stared at it, wished it would grow fins and swim off. She pulled a few translucent flakes away from the shiny skin and loaded them onto her fork, which hovered by her mouth before being put down untouched. She took her knife and popped the yolk. The pale yellow (was that a sign of freshness, the paleness?) poured lava like over the fish leaving volcanic trails. She supposed it looked perfect – to fishy egg eaters. She put a forkful of the newly drenched fish in her mouth. It took less than a second for her brain to register the cloying tepidity of the yolk, the slimy coolness of the haddock and send a message to her stomach, which heaved its rejection viciously. The waiter was over in a flash.

'Ees there something wrong with your fish Madame?'

'It's perfect' she said weakly, 'but not for me.'

He smiled sympathetically and stood over her holding the plate.

Alice wiped her mouth and took a sip of water. So much for nostalgia, she thought.

'I'm sorry' he said, discreetly removing the napkin. 'Can I get you another drink?'

'A glass of white maybe?' she said, with a watery smile.

⊦ ䷊ ⊣

Alice polished off a bread bun and the complementary bowl of vegetable soup that the waiter said would make her feel better. She sat quietly and watched the increasing activity in the dining room. Opposite, a corpulent man struggled to stay absorbed in his companion's opinions; his eyes darting uncontrollably often down the front of her gaping blouse. Another man – were all the men in the restaurant overweight? – took two bread buns from the waiter and balanced them neatly on the side of his soup bowl, but it was far from busy and there was little else to watch. She decided to have a coffee then leave, regretting her decision to come in the first place.

For want of anything better to do she fished in her bag for the gallery catalogue and flicked through the pages, skimming past Botticelli, Bruegel the Elder, Gainsborough and Turner – not that they weren't favourites, in a way, they were all favourites, but because her fingers seemed to be automatically searching for a certain picture. The image was smaller and the colours not quite right, but the impact was no less forceful: the barmaid, in 'A Bar at the Folies-Bergère.'

It was the first picture Graham took her to see at The Courtauld. It turned out that he wasn't a big Manet fan but the girl, the barmaid, bore a striking resemblance to Alice, he said. Alice could never see the likeness: the girl was much younger for one thing, her lips fuller, hair lighter, breasts larger, and over the years as Alice aged ahead of the barmaid, the similarities became increasingly tenuous. She looked at the picture now. The barmaid's eyes are permanently fixed, looking down at something, sad and distant. Reflected in the mirror behind her is a bustling scene of diners, a man in a top hat and the dangling feet of a trapeze artiste. Alice leant forward, closer to the picture, into it, and for a moment she and the barmaid became one. Her black garb became suitably Alice's. The young girl's uncertainty and deep sense of sadness echoed hers but mostly, they shared a feeling of isolation which left them both dislocated from what was going on around them. The deep sadness that lined Alice's heart burst and tears rolled down her cheeks onto the barmaid.

The waiter wasn't sure whether she was crying or not. He touched her elbow and when she looked up, he saw that she was. She took a moment to focus and when she registered the concern on his face, she smiled in gratitude. He placed a fresh napkin on the table and asked if she would like a coffee.

'Please,' she said, reaching down for her handbag, 'but I'll pop to the loo first.'

She set off across the dining room, bare footed, and a little wobbly legged.

She looked a mess – mascara down her cheeks, hair all over the place. She did what she could to tidy herself up: a touch of concealer, a dab of pink lipstick and a vigorous hair brushing, and then checked that she hadn't left anything lying around. A few more diners were arriving and she snaked her way back through the tables to her own. As she neared, she thought she must have made a mistake because a man was sitting at it. Confused, she scanned the room to no avail. And then she spotted her shoes lying on the floor.

'Your friend iz 'ere,' said the waiter, coming up beside her balancing a cafetiere on a small tray.

'Friend?' she said quizzically, not finding anything familiar about the stocky, grey haired man who had his back to her.

The waiter moved ahead to put the tray down and the man shifted so that Alice could see his profile. A funny feeling came over her: three years wasn't enough to have altered him hugely, but it was enough for Alice to do a double take before she was sure. It was like a blow to the stomach.

The room emptied, voices faded. Graham pushed his chair back, almost tipping it over, and stood up.

He was tall – of course he was, he hadn't shrunk, but he was heavier and he didn't move with the same crispness that Alice remembered. His hair was virtually grey, with only the tiniest hint of red to give you a clue as to how it used to be, and his skin sallow, yet there was more of it puffed up around his eyes which were the same pale aqua, but uncertain. It was the uncertainty that Alice found most shocking.

She was neither glad nor unhappy to see him. She ought to have been pleased because that was why she was there, but she felt numb.

expected him to say something in a fake French accent like he used to, such as 'What took you so long?' and hold his arms open, but he just stood – they both just stood, for what felt like an eternity.

'Graham,' she said, for the sake of saying something.

They sat at the same time. Alice plunged the cafetiere forcefully, spilling coffee grains onto the tablecloth. It was the kind of clumsiness that used to elicit a caustic rebuke, but he didn't appear to notice. She poured the coffee, dropped two roughly hewn sugar lumps in and stirred it, keeping her eyes on the cup.

'It's good to see you Alice,' he said. 'You look well.'

His voice was flat and diffident. Alice kept stirring.

'Yes, very well,' he said again.

Alice stirred on. Her eyes strayed to the lapels of his suit and lit upon a stain – a splash of coffee or soup perhaps, but a stain nonetheless. She felt like pointing it out.

'Thanks,' she said. She held her cup in two hands and began sipping, keeping her head low, and then felt rude because it was her table, so to speak, and Graham had nothing to drink.

'Can I get you something?' she asked, meeting his weary eyes for the first time.

'A glass of wine would be good.'

Alice smiled. She beckoned to the waiter and ordered a glass of Australian Sauvignon.

'How are you?' she said, curiosity getting the better of her.

He placed his hands on the tablecloth and splayed his fingers. They were the one piece of him that hadn't altered, so far as Alice could see. She had always loved his hands – long tapered fingers with immaculate nails, a wedding ring, of course. A shiver ran through her.

'I've been better,' he said.

'Oh?'

He shook his head in a dismissive gesture.

Was it Marcie or the kids, Alice wondered? Most probably work.

'Work,' he said eventually, looking at his hands in an accusatory fashion.

Graham's wine arrived. He tasted it and pursed his lips. The waiter frowned and Alice's heckles rose – taunting wine waiters was akin to bear baiting for Graham. She raised a hand in a calming gesture and the waiter backed off.

'It's really not that bad,' she said.

Graham shrugged. He twisted the stem of the wine glass between his fingers and asked her what she'd had to eat.

Alice wasn't sure whether to tell him about the smoked haddock or not.

'Soup,' she said, and then told him.

He gave a wry smile.

'I always knew you'd grow into it.'

Alice stared at him. 'Actually…' she began, and then couldn't be bothered. 'What's happened at work?' she said instead.

He had replaced an elderly man's right knee when it was the left that needed doing. The man recovered and there was no litigation involved, but it set off a train of investigation and mud-slinging.

Alice sat with her elbows on the table and listened attentively. She began to feel sorry for him, his reputation would have suffered, but the longer he went on, the more he criticised the management, theatre staff, x-ray, porters, technicians and nurses, the less she cared. His voice became strident and dogmatic. It grated on her and she recalled how exhausting he could be.

'Crikey,' she said. 'It's been tough.'

They didn't speak for a while. Alice caught sight of a red bus cutting a dash across the window. It was a sharp clear day and frost festooned the branches outside. Graham reached for the gallery catalogue and stood it on the table between them. His eyes moved between the open page and Alice's face. He looked at her with an intensity that made her uncomfortable. Don't say it, she thought.

'You still look like her,' he said. Unexpectedly, he reached out and tucked a strand of hair behind her ear. It felt like an assault and Alice spontaneously moved her head away. He looked aggrieved. 'You've not forgotten all the good times have you?'

Good times? Of course there had been good times; they had occupied her dreams for the last three years, but as she tried to recall them they slipped away and all she could remember was the waiting to fit into his life and the pain when they parted, the way he could ruin a meal by picking a fight with a waiter, or a trip to the opera by criticising the seats, and the crushing disappointment each time Marcie gave birth.

'I don't know what you expected,' she said. 'How is Marcie?'

He shifted uncomfortably.

'Oh, you know...'

Pregnant, thought Alice, shocked that she really didn't care.

'Memory,' she said, 'it's such a fickle thing, don't you think?'

She drifted down The Strand. Sadness hissed out and a sense of optimism stole in. She lengthened her stride and pushed her way through the Christmas crowds.

◐ ○ ◑

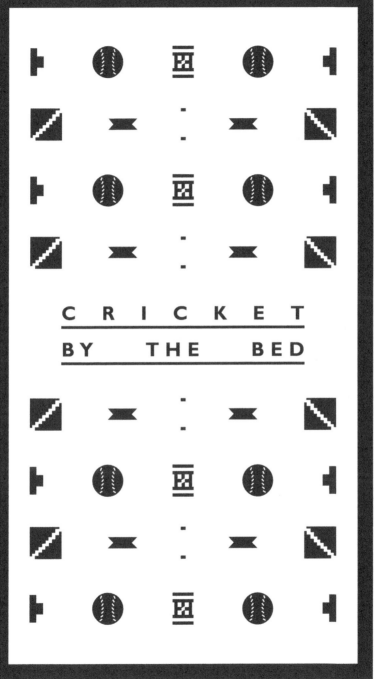

CRICKET

BY THE BED

Frank was reading the card when the doctor popped her head around the door. He'd found it by chance, the previous evening, and was smiling to himself: feeling faintly embarrassed about how cocky he'd been in his youth.

'I'm running a little late,' said the doctor. 'I'll be another half hour if that's okay?'

Frank felt relieved.

'I'll be here,' he said, and tucked the card away in his blazer pocket.

He took hold of May's hand and massaged her finger where the narrow gold ring was being swallowed up by water-logged tissues. Her eyes were shut, as they had been for the last month, and her breathing, shallow. Across the pillow her hair fanned out like filigree.

Frank squeezed May's hand gently and felt her warmth. He was frightened about May being cold: how could she be at peace if she was cold? May was a warm blooded woman. It nattered him.

Her first room in the home overlooked the railway line, but as soon as one at the back become available he asked for her to be moved into it. By that stage it was irrelevant to May, who didn't know if it was railway or canal through the window, but the calm water, with the occasional barge and stream of walkers along the tow path, was preferable.

'I don't want you to be cold love,' he said, and he moved as close to her as he could and rested his head on her chest. He melted into May's softness and the steady dull thump of her heartbeat soothed him and cleared his mind of worry. A strong, clear, sun warmed their faces. They slept.

Eventually a nurse came to check on May. Frank roused himself and when he sat up he ran his hands over his face and could feel the imprint the buttons on May's nightie had left on his cheek. He pointed them out to the nurse and they laughed. She gave him a cup of tea and to take his mind off the doctor's return, he switched on the television.

'It's the Test match,' he said to May with a wry smile.

If anything would induce May to linger on earth and delay being reunited with Andrew, it would be the final day of the Test. Cricket brought them together and kept them together – cricket and their children.

'At least they're wearing white,' said Frank. He was a traditionalist. He liked cricketers to be dressed in white, or at the very least cream, like he was, the first time May saw him.

'Do you remember my love, when we first met?' he whispered closely into her ear. 'Do you remember that baking hot day?'

He gave himself up to nostalgia and in his soft Geordie voice he told her for the last time how she had captivated him from day one.

⊦　⊠　⊦

'I knew where you were sitting all along. Avis's husband pointed you out from the balcony, and I could see you two girls chatting – Avis mostly – which was typical, and you listening and nodding and trying to take all that newness in.

'I could only see you from the back. You had an ethereal air about you, in your floaty white dress – your blonde hair spilling over your shoulders, and your skin – pure alabaster. I was willing you to turn round. I could see other people looking at you – but you didn't. You stayed forwards and it wasn't until we went out to field that I got the chance to see what all the fuss was about… and Christ, May – you were beautiful! You still are the most beautiful woman I know – those eyes, those huge cornflower eyes – when you smiled at me, I was lost. Lost…

'I'd been going to wait until after the match to say hello, but do you remember, at tea, I bumped into you coming out of the Ladies and Avis grabbed hold of me and said, 'Oh Frank, this is the lovely May who's coming out with us tonight,' and I said something like, 'How are you enjoying your first cricket match?' – not that you got chance to speak – Avis butted in. 'She's loving it – every minute – even your dropped catches,' she said, and you smiled, and I fell in love with the gap between your teeth and your dimples.

'When the match was over – and we were well and truly thrashed – Avis came flapping about, panicking that you had sunstroke – which you did – and she didn't have a clue what to do. I felt bloody awful – as if I'd damaged your perfection – you were already burning up at tea, but I didn't say anything because I thought you'd be embarrassed...

'Oh my love, you were in a sorry state. I can still see the look of horror on your face when I barged into the toilets with a bottle of Calamine Lotion and a load of cotton wool. Your shoulders were covered in blisters the size of old pennies and you'd just thrown up – but you were so brave – you might look fragile but you're made of gritty stuff. I dabbed it all over your shoulders, wincing each time you winced – covered my shirt in it too – and then – the only time in your life mind – you followed me like a lamb, and I ran you home in my Morris Traveller...

'When you disappeared inside and shut the door – I felt bereft. I hadn't felt that way about anyone else before.

'After work the next day I made you a Get Well Card. I drew a little picture of you, sitting in bed, all bandaged up. I had no idea that you kept it – only I found it last night – when I was doing some clearing out. I hope you don't mind. It was in a big old hat box in the bottom of your wardrobe. Here – let me get it out. Look, I wasn't much of an artist was I? Inside I wrote, "Pick you up next Sat at 8pm unless I hear otherwise" and I put my phone number on the back. What a cheek, eh? I'm surprised you came. But do you remember what you wrote inside the card? No? Well, next to my scrawl, you drew a big red tick and wrote,"Verrrry good idea. Think I'll marry this knight in shining armour!"

'I was going to stand the card on the windowsill but it wouldn't be right, would it? You've run out of getting well time... and I want you to be peaceful. We haven't had much peace since Andrew went…'

Frank composed himself.

He put the card back inside his pocket and patted it.

'It looks like we're all out and the Test's over,' he said, and he rested his head back on May's shoulder and waited.

WHAT DO YOU
THINK FRANK?

WHAT DO YOU THINK FRANK?

Val cut the sandwich into small squares and placed it by Frank's right hand. His teeth were loose and clacked together, but he ate it and drank the tea. In the toilet she helped unzip his fly and later went back to mop the floor.

The first month passed slowly. Frank knew he was lucky the stroke hadn't affected his speech, but he was frustrated. He spent hours staring at his left hand expecting it to suddenly spring back to life. He missed Sally and his grandson Zac. For six years he saw Zac twice a week, more sometimes, and then the Vicar took a job in Thurso. Coming so soon after May's death it was a double blow.

Frank was on Val's rota for the foreseeable future, Monday to Friday, morning and evening. It was someone different at the weekend. He got used to her coming and sat on the side of the bed until she arrived to help him dress, left side first. If he got it wrong she was quick to correct. She had a blunt way with words that Frank secretly approved of. He ate his breakfast in the kitchen and then watched her as he stroked his left hand with his right and stretched out his fingers. She moved quickly – seemed to know instinctively where things lived, and as she rushed, she talked, about her kids and the donkeys. She rented a small field and kept four of them safe from the knacker's yard. She rose early to tend them and went again in the evening. Her hands were calloused. On the top of her arm was a moon shaped scar from a donkey bite. She showed it off with pride, like a rosette. When Frank didn't talk, she didn't appear bothered. She was the kind of person it would be easy to become dependent on.

Val's bad-luck face was no accident. It came from her parents who came from Bramley and was shaped by her father's serrated tongue, a brother's death, a baby when she was fifteen, her husband's disappearance and the constant threat from drug dealers. She never knew her grandparents so presumed they hadn't fared too well in life either. It didn't help that she smoked – deep lines circled her mouth and her cheeks were a mass of broken veins.

What set her apart from her ancestors was that Val was a grafter who fought her way through life's miseries, putting them behind her like a batsman knocking sixes over his shoulder. She was always hopeful that her lot in life would improve. For years she cobbled together cash-in-hand jobs but once her youngest was at senior school she got a job doing home care. Compared to some of the poor sods she visited, she was lucky.

It took a month to win Frank over. One day she gave him an old toothbrush.

'Someone told me that if you brush your hand with this – gently like – it'll help bring the nerves back to life.'

Frank picked up the brush and gave it a go, gingerly at first, and then longer sweeps, from elbow to hand. He didn't think it was going to do any good, and was about to tell her so, when she dropped a bottle of milk on the floor. Shards of glass clattered on the tiles and milk coursed along the cracks in-between, spraying the cupboard fronts. Her pale green uniform, always pressed, always spotless, was patterned with expanding jade spots that she frantically tried to brush off.

'Bugger!' she stormed. 'Bugger, bugger, bugger!'

Frank shrank into his chair. Val grabbed the mop and set about swishing it furiously from side to side, squeezing greyed milk into the bucket and swishing it again, all the while muttering, 'blood and sand.' Finished at last, she collapsed opposite Frank and began to sob.

Frank raced through what he knew about Val. He stretched his right arm over and patted her shoulder.

'I'm sorry,' he said. 'Is it one of the donkeys?'

She shook her head vigorously. Words escaped between gulps.

'I came in from work one day last September and George was sitting in the kitchen. He had that big crooked smile on his face. I thought he had a job or something and was about to give him a hug, when he said he'd joined up. I didn't know what he meant. "Joined what?" I said, and he said, "The Infantry." I told him he could go back down and un-join, but he wouldn't, the little sod. Said he wanted to go to Afghanistan. Wanted to get away from here. From the dealers, I think, but he wouldn't admit it.

'Ritchie and Ali came in and he told them. You should have seen the look of respect on Ritchie's face. And everyone he told looked like that. They smacked him on the back and he hadn't even gone anywhere. Anyhow, I'm taking him tomorrow,' she said wearily. 'Over to Catterick so I won't be here. They'll send somebody else.'

Val looked despondent.

'Were you in the war Frank?'

'Not abroad but my brothers Ken and Joe went.'

'Did it change them?'

Frank spoke without thinking.

'Killed Ken,' he said, 'and changed Joe.'

Frank didn't like it when Val couldn't come and replacements were sent. He tried to be more independent and one day Val noticed that he had made his own breakfast. She looked tired but set about tidying, talking as usual.

'I told him to keep his head down and to listen. Listen, listen, listen, I said. Do what you're told and listen. Forty have gone from The King's Own. You should have seen his kit bag, all that water and radio stuff. I couldn't even lift it. He rang Tuesday morning at four-a-bleedin-clock. He can have twenty minutes of calls a week but he only had seven. Said there was a queue. Do you think he'll call again Frank?'

Frank nodded.

'I hope so. I knew it was him cos it was a foreign number. He talked very fast. Said he was in Afghan but couldn't say any more. He was shaking when they landed. You would, wouldn't you Frank? Shake. They flew in a Chinook. Have you heard of a Chinook Frank?'

Vietnam, thought Frank, and nodded.

'We can send him as many shoeboxes as we want as long as they don't weigh more than 2kgs. I took three to the post yesterday. They go to Camp Bastion. Have you heard of Camp Bastion Frank? I didn't have to pay! Imagine that. Free! It's good to know our taxes are being spent on something useful.'

Frank smiled.

'Chuffin' heck!' she said. 'You're in fine fettle,' and went to vac the lounge.

News from George trickled through. He said they were going from village to village teaching the locals how to be soldiers, that they filmed the terrain as they went and passed it on to the teams who followed. He said he'd lost weight and was always hungry. He sometimes said, "We've had a trying day". When he said this Val wanted to ask him if he'd killed anyone, but she held back, the thought was unbearable and anyway, he wouldn't have been able to say. Details were scant.

Frank asked the Saturday lady to buy things for a shoebox. He knew from Val that chocolate, Pot-noodles and small boxes of cereal, (eaten with goat's milk) went down well. When Val came on Monday morning he was sitting stroking his arm with the toothbrush, a shoebox in the middle of the table.

'For George,' he said.

Val's hand went to her throat. 'You shouldn't have done that. Chicken's his favourite. He'll be right pleased. I'll send it with our Ali's this afternoon.' She put the lid on and patted it. 'You're a goodun Frank. What's your news today?'

Frank's stock reply was 'nothing new,' but as he felt mythered and admired Val's openness he told her what was preying on his mind.

'Sally's not called for a fortnight.'

'Chuffin' kids. Couldn't you just wring their necks?' she said, tipping her head to one side. 'Give her a call. I would.'

Frank looked aghast. It was Sally's job to call him.

'Go on Frank. You've nothing to lose.'

'That vicar,' he said with uncharacteristic vehemence, 'took Sally and Zac to the back of beyond. If I could get my hands round his neck I'd break it.' He made an exaggerated wringing motion as best he could. It was hard to say which of the two of them was most surprised.

'Not a Vicar, Frank,' said Val. 'That could be a bit awkward.'

⊦ ⊠ ⊣

Frank found himself worrying about George. Val reported that he rang three or four times a week, usually in the middle of the night. Six days went by and Val looked increasingly haggard as the weekend approached.

'Do you think they'd send someone round in the middle of the night or wait until the morning – or phone me – or send a letter – or worse, a whatsit, an email? What if I saw it on the telly first?' she said, and immediately switched it off in case there was a news bulletin.

It was the railway police when Andrew died, but Frank couldn't bear to think about that.

'Do they still send telegrams?' he said.

When George did ring the news tumbled out of Val.

'He said there's been a set-to. They got no warning. A local lad lost his legs and my George was first there. Imagine that. The poor sod. He's got a big sore on his back and it's boiling hot. Next week he's back training villagers. He asked what his mates were up to and I told him, hanging around doing nothing or selling drugs. I don't know Frank; I'm beginning to think he's better off there than he is here! He's still starving and oh, he said thanks for the shoeboxes.'

Frank gave a lopsided smile.

'Sally called last night.'

'Oh?'

'She won't be coming for Christmas. Zac's revising for his exams.'

He looked at Val. He didn't see lines and veins any more; he saw compassion.

'Well, you'll come to us then,' she said. 'Ritchie 'll pick you up.'

⊠

Frank opted to stay at home. He hoped that May, wherever she was, couldn't see him. He toyed with the plated-up meal that Ritchie brought down and watched the Queen's speech. The phone rang. Most likely Sally, he thought.

'Happy Christmas Granddad,' said Zac.

It was only when Frank heard his voice that he realised how much he missed him.

'It can't be Zac,' he said. 'Zac's not Scottish.'

They talked about Christmas presents, football and exams.

'Is your Mum there?' said Frank eventually.

'She's er,' Zac hesitated, 'got a bug.'

'A bug? Oh! Tell her to get better soon. And your Dad, where's he?'

'I don't know.'

'At church?'

'He might be.'

'Where else would he be?' joked Frank.

'God knows!' said Zac. 'There's no art class on Christmas day.'

Frank felt uneasy – he hadn't heard Zac take the Lord's name before and the conversation ended soon afterwards. It was his tone of voice that bothered him – angry, resentful, bitter? He couldn't pin it down. He practised walking slowly round the house using one stick and when he tired he sat down and concentrated on touching the fingertips on his left hand to his thumb. He nodded off and was woken by the back door being flung open.

'A turkey and stuffing sandwich for your tea,' said Val, waving it in front of him. 'George did Christmas yesterday. He had to catch his own chicken and ate it with carrots and a few spuds,' she laughed. 'Imagine that! He must be growing up, my George. He never so much as peeled a spud when he was home. Anyhow, guess what?' She brought her face level with Frank's. 'I've some good news. He's coming home – not right away – he'll have to debrief in Cyprus for a while first. But I don't care. I'm so happy Frank, I can't tell you how happy I am. We'll have a party Frank and you'll have to come.'

She took his head in her hands and kissed him on the forehead.

⊢ ▣ ⊣

A month later the first real snow of winter arrived. It dragged on and Frank began to wonder if it would ever warm up. He got into the habit of watching at the window for Val. She parked as near as she could and walked the rest of the way. As soon as he saw her he put the kettle on. Her hands were always freezing when she arrived.

'I think it might be starting to thaw,' she said as she unpacked the shopping. 'And that's good, because,' she paused dramatically, 'my George is back in Cyprus! He doesn't want a party but we'll have to have one. You'll come, won't you Frank. You sent him all those boxes and he's desperate to meet you.'

Frank didn't know about the party but he shared Val's relief.

'Wonderful,' he said. 'Home in one piece.'

'It's still a week but that's not long is it? And no arguing Frank, I'm going to give you a shower today. No ifs and buts. Today Frank. It must be a month since you had one.'

'Not with those hands,' he said. But she did. Afterwards she left him dressing and went to make his lunch. When she came back upstairs she looked flustered.

'Zac's downstairs. He wants to see you.'

It was a year since Frank saw Zac. They hugged awkwardly. Val looked suspicious.

'Right then, I'll go if things are OK,' she said.

Frank nodded.

'Don't forget your Granddad's eighty-two, and he's a bit slow – not in the head, he's sharp as a tack in his head, but on his feet...' She threw Zac a warning glance and left.

Zac looked washed out. No daylight in Scotland, thought Frank.

'This is unexpected,' he said.

'It's a surprise.'

'It is that. Does your Mum know you're here?'

Zac shuffled on his chair.

'She's not at home.'

Frank frowned.

'And your Dad?'

'He's not my Dad,' said Zac.

It never occurred to Frank that the Vicar might not be Zac's father yet he knew Zac was telling the truth. It explained why Zac bore no resemblance to him whatsoever.

'Where is your mum?'

'At Aunty Harriet's for the week.'

He glanced at the backpack by the door.

'It looks like you're staying?'

'Can I Granddad?'

Zac moved his stuff into the spare room. He phoned his mum to tell her where he was but refused to ring the Vicar. Sally said she would call him. He walked to Brett's to get fish and chips and then went for a sleep. He'd been hitch-hiking for two days.

Frank's head was spinning. If the vicar wasn't Zac's father, who was? He wondered if Zac knew and if so, how he found out. All in the fullness of time, no doubt. He would enjoy his grandson's company until Sunday when he would go home.

⊦ ䷄ ⊦

Val was having none of it.

'It won't do him any favours lying in bed all day. He needs to be out in the fresh air, not in here brooding. He can come with me to sort the donkeys. That'll get him up in the morning and out in the evening. Don't be mollycoddling the boy Frank.'

Yesterday Zac didn't get up until midday and then lay on the sofa watching the television.

'Tell him to dress up warm and I'll pick him up at six. I've got spare Wellies.'

⊢ 亘 ⊣

Zac went with Val. He looked unimpressed.

Two days and the house felt quiet without him. Frank sat in May's chair feeling thoroughly miserable – he missed her more than ever.

The following day Zac was up early waiting for Val. And the next. On Friday he stayed with the donkeys all day. Saturday was George's party. Zac helped his granddad dress.

'So you like donkeys now?' said Frank.

'Yep.

'Don't turn your back on them. Have you seen the bite on Val's arm?'

'That was Casper. Val said he was starved when he came to her.'

Frank lifted his left foot and put it into the leg hole of his trousers. He pulled them up with his right hand and waited whilst Zac tucked in his shirt and fastened them. He tied his tie.

'You like Val?' said Frank.

'Yeah. She's cool. She was ecstatic yesterday when George came home.'

Frank must have misunderstood. He thought George wasn't back until today.

'He didn't want to be in the house so he came up to see the donkeys. He's used to being outside.' Zac became increasingly animated. 'He's in the King's Own and he's seen loads of stuff. He's doing another tour but hasn't told Val yet.'

Frank didn't like that. Val would be distraught. He looked at the shirt and tie in the mirror. He hadn't socialised since before the stroke and felt uncomfortable about going to the party. It crossed his mind to ring with an excuse, except it would be rude to Val, and Zac seemed set on it.

Ritchie pulled up in Val's car, his usual dopey expression replaced with a huge grin.

'It's all kicking off,' he said. 'He's skinny as owt! Come on, grab my arm and we'll get off.'

Ritchie and Zac sat in the front. Frank couldn't hear what they said but it was obvious that George's return was exciting them. It was understandable. He felt something similar when Joe came home at the end of the war – relieved he was safe, wishing that he had been allowed to go. As the details emerged he felt differently. He looked at Zac and felt anxious.

Val's house stood at the top of a cul-de-sac. It was draped with a huge 'Welcome Home' banner. He hoped she'd get the chance to use it again if George went back.

⊦ 🏛 ⊣

The following day he watched Val scuttle round the kitchen.

'It's a wonder I'm here,' she said. 'It was well-gone midnight when they went and then there was the tidying to do. You looked to be having a good time Frank?'

He did have a good time. Second to George he was centre of attention. A string of people chatted to him and brought food and drink over. It was what May would have called 'a rough and ready affair,' but none the worse for it. Frank tired early and Ritchie ran him home. Sleep eluded him. All he could see was Zac's worshiping face hanging on George's every word.

'He was having a right good time. Was one of the last to leave.'

'He's having a lie in. It won't do him any harm. He's back to Scotland tomorrow.'

Val put two mugs of tea on the table.

'You'll miss him Frank, won't you? Maybe he can come again at Easter or in the summer. That'd be good.'

Frank had already considered this.

'I don't know what's going on,' he said wearily. 'Sally says it's not a conversation to have over the phone.'

'I thought you...' Val looked amazed. 'The vicar's having an affair with a woman called Sheena from his art class and your Sally found out. There was a mother and father of a row and the vicar told Sally that he knew Zac wasn't his son. Zac heard it all and hey presto, here we are.'

Frank flinched. No wonder Zac wasn't in a hurry to go home.

At lunchtime Frank went slowly upstairs. Zac's bed was made and his bag gone. There was no need for a note.

⊙ O ⊙

A   GAME   OF

CONSEQUENCES

A GAME OF CONSEQUENCES

A Shamefaced girl
met
Her father
in
The bluebell woods next to the house.
She said to him,
'I'm so pleased you've come to the baby naming.
Today is all about welcoming Julia and introducing
her to everyone. We want her to choose her own
religion when she's old enough.'
He said to her,
'I'll go and see if your mother will get out of the car.'
What happened next?
She didn't. She wound the window down and
cooed at Julia. She hid her face from her daughter
behind a floral pink dupatta.
What happened in the end?
On Julia's second birthday her grandmother arrived
with a dish of kebabs. The smell of coriander and
cumin was enough to make a shamefaced girl weep.

Marcie

met

Alice

at

A perfume counter in Selfridges.

Marcie said,

'It's Alice isn't it? It's a sickly scent that one. I always
knew when Graham had been with you.'

Alice said,

'I'm sorry.' (And she meant it)

What happened next?

They went to the café on the third floor. Alice paid.

(It was the least she could do.)

What happened in the end?

Marcie had the baby. It wasn't Graham's, which
made Alice smile.

Wendy

met

Pete

at

The inquest into Andrew Hasting's death.

She said to him,

'Andrew was my patient. I'm retired now but would you like to get together and have a talk sometime? It might be helpful.'

He said to her,

'I've got a model railway in the garage. Do you want to see it?'

What happened next?

Wendy went to the garage. It took thirty-seven visits before Pete flicked the switch and sent the train past the Friesians.

What happened in the end?

Pete got a job in the model railway shop at York station. He sold Humbrol colours to his heart's content. Wendy was happy to rewrite the end of her career.

The Vicar

met

Sheena

at

Life drawing classes.

He said to her,

'I think you've got a beautiful face and beautiful
curves. The Lord would approve of you showing
them off.'

She said to him,

'Ooh, do you think so Vicar?'

(She was thick as two short planks)

What happened next?

It made the Nationals. Sally packed her bags and
moved south.

What happened in the end?

It was a lonely parish with no parishioners.

Harriet

met

Halisi and Aminah

at

Joe's funeral.

Harriet said to Aminah,

'Come on darling. Sit between your mum and me.

We'll get through this together.'

Halisi said,

'Am I the only one wearing a hat?'

What happened next?

Noisy Kenyan weeping and much head turning.

What happened in the end?

A once-only snorkeling holiday to Watamu Bay.

Fish and coral weren't Harriet's thing.

Zac

met

Hassan

on

The Nefertiti, sailing up The Nile.

Zac said,

'You probably don't remember my mum Sally. You
had a one-night stand with her twenty-two years
ago.

Hassan said,

'Big Sally?'

What happened next?

They leant against the rails watching the world slip
by – huts, children and animals. They kept their
thoughts to themselves.

What happened in the end?

No tourists. No income. Zac set up a monthly
standing order to The Bank of Luxor.

Frank met his maker, aged 92.
He lived long enough to see Zac make the rank
of Major, and Sally remarry.
Val retired from home-care and expanded the
donkey sanctuary with Lottery funding. George
helped run it. It was amazing how much he could
do with one hand.

Lightning Source UK Ltd.
Milton Keynes UK
UKOW07f0524091215

264406UK00016B/241/P